CULLE NT

IN THE

Dry Woods

RIVER
THE
BOOKS

© Cullene Bryant 2005

River Books and The Books Collective acknowledge the ongoing support of the Canada Council for the Arts and the Alberta Foundation for the Arts for our publishing programme. We also acknowledge the assistance of the Edmonton Arts Council.

Editors for the Press: Candas Jane Dorsey, Timothy J. Anderson.
Cover art by Erica Grimm.
Cover design by Bella Totino of Totino Busby Design Ltd.
Page design and typography by Ana M. Anubis of Ingénieuse Productions, Edmonton.
Printed by Priority Printing Ltd., Edmonton.

The text was set in Monotype's *Bembo*, which was modeled on typefaces cut by Francesco Griffo for Aldus Manutius' printing of *De Aetna* in 1495 in Venice. In 1929, Stanley Morison supervised the design of *Bembo* for the Monotype Corporation. *Bembo* is a fine text face because of its well-proportioned letterforms, functional serifs, and lack of peculiarities; the italic is modeled on the handwriting of the Renaissance scribe Giovanni Tagliente. Books and other texts set in *Bembo* can encompass a large variety of subjects and formats because of its quiet classical beauty and high readability. Titles are set in URW's *Washington Light*, a grotesque geometric sans serif. Page dingbats are from Adobe's *Zapf Dingbats*.

In keeping with our commitment to preserving the world's ancient forests and the responsible use of resources, this book was printed on Everest 80lb. text, an ancient forest-friendly, 100% post-consumer recycled paper.

Published in Canada by River Books, an imprint of
    The Books Collective
    214-21, 10405 Jasper Avenue
    Edmonton, Alberta T5J 3S2.
    Telephone (780) 448-0590   Fax (780) 448-0640

Library and Archives Canada Cataloguing in Publishing

Bryant, Cullene
    In the dry woods / Cullene Bryant.

ISBN 1-894880-04-8

I. Title.
PS8553.R912I5 2004   C813'.54   C2004-905907-6

In the Dry Woods

Cullene Bryant

Dedicated to
Alex and Delyana
Rhiannon and Jason.

Somewhere blooms the blossom of parting and bestrews
evermore over us pollen which we breathe:
even in the most-coming wind we breathe parting.

Rilke

I. Out of the Storm

Unmeeting

Missa Solemnis

Diva

New York, New York,

Jazz Man

Saved

Wild Life in the Canadian Wilderness

II. Through the Jungle

Promise

Two Sisters

Head Hunters

Bahala Na

III. In the Dry Woods

I
Out of the Storm

Night comes quickly
but the snow gives off so much shine
it's not as dark as where you are
the big trees leaning in

Joan Crate

Unmeeting

Neuschwanstein:

I caught my breath. Nothing had prepared me for the splendour of the castle. We had walked halfway up a green mountain before we saw it, hidden in the woods. The spires seemed to graze the sky. "It's gorgeous, Freidmann," I said.

"I wanted to show it to you," he answered.

We were standing shoulder to shoulder, gazing up at the graceful edifice, and I wished he would take my hand. Every woman should be brought here by her lover, I thought.

"See the swan decoration at the very top? This motif is repeated many times on the inside," he said playing the tour guide again. I took a picture of him standing in front of the drawbridge.

Editor's Comment: A good symbol. The exterior of the castle with its formidable drawbridges, barricades etc. represents Freidmann's ultimate invincibility.

He continued to lecture me. "The swan is a central symbol in Wagner's operas. He and the emperor who built this castle were very close friends. Some of the paintings inside the castle depict scenes from his works."

"I've never been to one of Wagner's operas but I'd love to see *The Flying Dutchman.*"

"Why?"

"Because the characters find salvation through love."

"I never listen to Wagner. He was greatly admired by Hitler. Many of us in Germany feel his music should be banned."

He was angry about the war again. If it made him feel that way I didn't want to go inside the castle. Instead, I wanted to run down the hill, run to the American beaches where Freidmann seemed like a different man.

New York:

We met in New York at the International Conference for Pastoral Care. I was there covering the story for the *United Church Observer.* He was a Lutheran minister, divorced like me and living with his teenage daughter. He sat in the middle of the room and a little apart from everyone else, unmoved by the commotion. Dressed in a glossy black leather jacket he shone like molten rock.

Editor's Comment: Overwriting

Perhaps that's what drew me to him. He seemed solid, secure, at peace. I needed a resting place. After my husband, Paul, left, life was a rocky sea and I, shipwrecked. The first thing I did was go back to school and embark on an MA. in creative writing. I supported myself by doing some freelance journalism. That was how I came to be in New York.

But there were no castles in the United States, only lights. I was mesmerized by them, pressed against the rails of a ferry boat and gazing at the city's skyline. They bobbed and glistened like lanterns in a Mandarin garden. We were returning from a day at the beach where we had swam and made love in the sand at sunset.

Editor's Comment: Must it happen at sunset?

That day at the beach, he swept over me and I was pulled into his being like a helpless swimmer caught in ocean currents. My sister who lives on Long Island said, "The ocean never drowned anyone. The swimmers kill themselves. If they can float with the tide, eventually, they'll be washed back on the shore. But if they fight they get into trouble and drown." Afterwards, he rolled over and lay beside me holding my hand. Then, we washed each other, standing knee-deep in the ocean.

Rottenberg:

The afternoon I arrived in Germany, he picked me up from the airport in his Mercedes Benz and we sped along the *Autobahn.* "We'll stay in a castle tonight," he said.

"How romantic," I smiled.

Our bedroom was in the turret and when I went to look out the window I saw a brilliant blue peacock strutting in the courtyard.

"This place is too beautiful," I said.

He got ready for bed in an orderly fashion, unpacked and laid out his clothes for the morning, cleaned his teeth, showered. It was as if we had been together for the year. I covered myself quickly while he turned out the light and moved towards me. I had gained weight that winter. "I've missed you," I said. I was so eager for his body against me and in me that I closed my eyes and could hardly speak or move. I waited for his response, words of yearning.

"You feel good," he said and when he was finished turned away to sleep.

In the morning I awakened to a hundred birds singing. I lay there, patiently waiting for him to touch me again. Just as I reached over, he pulled himself out of bed and without glancing at me started dressing for the day. "I want to drive down the Romantic Highway. There are two or three medieval towns which you will love. We're quite fortunate in Germany that these weren't destroyed by the bombs," he said.

I went into the bathroom to dress. After a quick breakfast of cheese and bread we were once again in his car.

Fischen:

The next night we slept in his uncle's house. I complained bitterly but Freidmann treated my desire lightly. He explained that after his father was killed he was raised by this man. "It would be quite impossible for me to pass by without paying my respects. Appearances are very important here in Germany. He's the head of my family."

"We have so little time together," I said.

"I'll sneak into your room in the middle of the night," he laughed. "Don't worry."

But he didn't. I stayed awake listening to the wind rattle the shutters and remembered our time together in New York.

Editor's Comment: Again, the incurable romantic

Suddenly there was an explosion under my window. Too loud for a car to be backfiring and too deep and hollow for a gun shot. I listened for more noise. Nothing. Then ripping through the air, a second bang. I leapt to the window and heard a third crash followed by a blue flame. It must be small bombs exploding, I thought. Here I am in Germany. I can't even speak the language and we're being attacked. Pride kept me from running into Freidmann's room and I shivered in bed until morning.

Editor's Comment: Thank God!

When I went down for breakfast, Freidmann and the old man were sitting at the table. "Did you hear the noise last night?" he said.

"Yes. I was terrified. What was it?"

"My uncle says there was a wedding here yesterday. It's a custom that after the bride and groom have retired for the night their friends fill balloons with gasoline. They light them so that they will explode in the air over the bedroom of the bride and groom."

The old man's eyes twinkled as he waited for my laughter and a nod of understanding. I could tell he loved the story. I gave him a crisp smile and secretly hated the young bride who knew a tenderness that I was not allowed to give or receive.

Editor's Comment: Is this much pain, desire intrinsic to the modern single woman of the nineties. What happened to the hard-won autonomy and independence of the feminist movement?

New York:

I had to interview the speakers at night because we skipped most of the conference together. Freidmann refused to accommodate himself to a schedule. We discovered a jazz joint and I found out he shared my passion for American Blues. He didn't know much about progressive Jazz but loved the idea of improvisation. As he tapped his foot and sipped wine, I thought he enjoyed feeling somewhat dissolute. He hated order, especially when it was imposed from the outside. "Following rules is so important, even in Germany today. It's that sort of mentality which created the Third Reich," he said. As he spoke his cheeks flushed and I sensed the deep shame he felt about his country's history.

When at last the conference was over I mailed my material to the editor, and Freidmann and I took a couple of weeks' holidays and toured museums and art galleries. His camera was full of me. I felt like a New York model as he flashed one photo after another. Later, back in Toronto, missing him and lonely, I received a thick packet of pictures. It seemed there was another woman staring back at me, flowers in her hair, transformed and beautiful.

Toronto/Edmonton:

Somehow, after meeting him in New York, I survived another hard and lonely year. Since there was a dearth of teaching jobs in Toronto, I applied out west and was accepted as an instructor of creative writing at Grant MacEwan College. That meant leaving my home, my roots, my family.

When I arrived in Edmonton the summer was over and the magpies remained, the only birds in the city, alone and squawking. Winter was already snapping at everyone's heels. People told me to carry a candle in my car because it would give off enough heat to keep a person from freezing to death in a snowstorm and they argued about cures for frostbite and said how all the roses in my garden would die if I didn't see that they were covered. The space frightened me. If I got lost on Mount Pleasant Avenue in Toronto I could turn the car into the driveway of a friendly neighbourhood drugstore or pizza parlour and ask for directions. But I could drive down the Whitemud Freeway forever and never even see a gas station. I missed the jostle of the crowd on the Bloor subway. Even in West Edmonton Mall there was so much space people kept a respectable distance from each other. As the winter wore on, I became more lonely, gained weight and grew more wrinkles around my eyes. Then the *Observer* phoned and asked me to cover another story, this time in Tübingen. I was to interview Moltmann, a well known German theologian on nuclear disarmament. I wrote to Freidmann.

He answered my letter, apparently thrilled that we could be together again. "I'd like to see the Berlin wall," I had written.

"That's much too depressing," he wrote back. "Let me take you down the Romantic Highway. It's a road that meanders through towns which date back to the middle ages. I'll take you on a tour of castles." I began having fantasies of a courtship carried on back and forth across the ocean and toyed with the idea of signing up for German lessons in case I should end up living in that country.

When the winter was over the west spread herself before me with all the fire and sweetness of the prairie flowers. Driving across the flat land to the mountains, all I could see to the left and right of me was warm brown earth like an undulating ocean. The prairies reached out and drew me down, embraced and anchored me in the soil, moist and fecund, as a woman's body holds a man. At the end of that summer the world seemed full of hope and new longing. I flew to Germany.

Dinkelsbuehl:

"There's the city wall," he said as we got out of the car. "Let's climb up and look at the view."

By this time I was tired of the cobblestones and was tripping on them. He wasn't taking any pictures and posed only when I asked him. Ahead of us was a young mother with two little girls playing about her skirts. Her husband walked beside her carrying their baby boy. Because their hands and arms were so full of children they couldn't touch. But their shoulders brushed against each other while they walked. He smiled at her and she looked up laughing. She's not very beautiful, I thought. She wears no makeup and her teeth protrude a little underneath her thick lips. "You must take a picture. See. They are dressed in Bavarian clothes," said Freidmann.

I had already noticed the full blue skirts and the white crinolines and pretty blonde braids of the children. But that is not what had impressed me. No. It was the pleasure that she took in his gazing on her and the joy they felt in their love. I was jealous and blocked her way on the narrow street. I snapped my camera with a loud click while the children squealing like frightened sparrows ran and hid in the folds of their mother's dress.

Nurnberg:

He wouldn't stop talking about the war even as we stood in the city square. "I want to take you to where the Nurnberg trials were held."

"Then we can see the Berlin wall?" I said with a touch of sarcasm.

We were standing in front of the cathedral and watching the clock with its little mechanical figures. At the sound of the chimes they appeared and marched in a circle. "Some day documents will be produced that will exonerate Germany and prove that the Allies were just as much at fault in starting the war," he said with passion.

I bit my tongue. He had told me in New York how his mother sent him to the prison before her husband was shipped to France. As a boy he travelled for miles with a few of his father's personal effects, pajamas, a sweater, his toothbrush, a few family photographs. He remembered how he sat by the railroad track and cried. That was the last time he saw his father. A glimpse through the bars.

Editor's Comment: With the description of the Canadian West and the German towns I sometimes wonder if I'm reading a travelogue instead of a short story!

Neuschwanstein:

"You'll love this castle," he said. "It's my favourite place in Germany."

Surely this is the place he'll at last take me in his arms, confess his longing and loneliness, beg me to leave my home and country. All great writers achieve a new perspective in another land; didn't Margaret Laurence write her first book of short stories in Africa? Instead, Freidmann recited the history of the castle. "It was built by Emperor Ludwig the Second. Some say he was a philosopher who needed a beautiful place like this for study and meditation. Those people think in a fit of romantic despair he drowned himself. Others say he was a cruel despot who unmercifully taxed the peasants and drove them to hard labour. They killed him by drowning. His death will always be a mystery."

Poor Freidmann. I watched him gazing up at the spires, encircled by a rainbow. (There had been a sunshower as we climbed the hill.) No wonder he's drawn to this place and has been so aloof, I thought. He's like the emperor who stayed inside his castle and watched the artist paint the pictures of the Lohengrin Saga instead of walking among the peasants and getting to know them.

Editor's Comment: Yes. He does have problems with intimacy. But must she make excuses for him implying he is like the German poet / emperor / mystic, Ludwig?

On our last evening, he took me to an historic inn for dinner. "The mail coach used to stop here, to change horses," he said. We ate a meal of German sausages and beer. While coffee was being served he explained that he had to spend the rest of the night with his daughter. I had forgotten he lived with her.

"She's writing her final exams and is very upset. I want her to study in the States."

"What does she want to be?" I asked trying to muster a show of interest.

"A doctor. I hope she does well."

"You're the one who wants to go to the States," I said. "You were different there."

"Yes. I know. I love America. There's too much order, here. Too depressing."

Editor's Comment: Here the writer shows her incredible naiveté. The protagonist actually believes he's spending the night with his daughter

When we were finished dinner he took my bags upstairs to the room. "You'll be comfortable here? Don't you think it's good for you to be alone for a night to get yourself organized? You'll be busy in Tübingen doing your interview."

"Don't worry. I have some things to do. Laundry and so on."

"*Gute nacht,*" he kissed me lightly on the lips.

I wanted to fall on him, beg him to remember all that we once shared, demand an explanation. Instead I said, "Thank you for the dinner," and quietly closed the door.

Editor's Comment: I wonder, do you know any strong women?

That night I dreamed I was driving through the prairies. My car stalled and I froze to death.

The next morning after a quick breakfast he took me to the train station.

The bags were heavy but he carried them easily and with a smile as he did when he first met me. A young university student was sharing a compartment and since he spoke English Freidmann asked if he would see that I got off at the right stop. Then he took me back down to the platform to say goodbye. To my surprise he kissed me and when I looked up at him there were tears in his eyes. He said something which I couldn't hear because the whistle blew. I scurried back to my seat and rushed to the window for a last glimpse of him. He was stuffing his handkerchief back into his pocket. He saw me, waved and smiled. As the train began to move I realized that was how the soldiers and their wives strained for a last glimpse of their loved ones: the Germans, French, Canadians, British. We're all the same.

Then his figure receded quickly into the distance even though I stood on tiptoe to see him, a tiny dot fast diminishing.

Editor's Comment: fair ending but verging on the romantic — last kiss etc. Try again.

When the waiter brought the cheque I insisted on paying. "My treat," I said. After a brief argument he agreed and I stood trembling with rage in front of the cashier. "How can he spend our last night with his daughter?" I wondered.

"Did you enjoy the dinner?" asked the cashier.

"Yes, thank you. It's a lovely old inn." I was having trouble making change as I carefully counted the unfamiliar silver.

"Too bad you're not staying for the night."

"You have rooms?"

"Of course, this is an inn."

I glanced back at Freidmann who was buckling up his coat. "I'll take one, a single." Just as she handed me the keys he came over.

"What are you doing?" he said.

"I've got a room for the night."

"But I was going to get you nice place in the suburbs close to my house so I could drive you to the train tomorrow."

"Please don't worry."

"As you like."

He carried my bag upstairs and asked, "You'll be comfortable here? See you in the morning."

There was an awkward moment when I thought he was going to kiss me.

Then he was gone. I closed the door of my little room. I didn't cry. I unpacked. Then, I pulled out the chair from the desk that sat under the window and gazed out at the moon, the same moon that would be shining over Edmonton when I returned home.

I rummaged in my suitcase for a pad of paper. I began writing this story. I worked all night because I knew I could sleep on the train. In the morning I settled the bill and left a carefully worded thank-you note for Freidmann.

Editor's Comment: Here the writer goes overboard in an attempt to look like a feminist, even thought it is apparent she is not.

The taxi driver spoke good English and when we got to the station went out of his way to direct me to the right platform. I boarded the train, and tried not to notice the woman ahead of me who clung tearfully to her husband as they kisssed goodbye. I settled into my seat and the train pulled out. We sped by narrow streets and old buildings crowded together.

When I get back home summer will be over, I thought as I leaned back in my seat and settled in for a nap. Flashes of sun played on my closed eyelids and I could see the familiar landscape, clean and spacious, covered in white gleaming snow.

Missa Solemnis

The altar boy holds the long taper high in the air, his extended arm quivering, standing on tiptoe in order to reach the top of the white Paschal candle. The priest meets the coffin at the door, says a brief prayer and proceeds with the mourners down the aisle. He approaches the altar table and bows to the crucifix while the men place their burden near the lighted candle. Then he turns towards the congregation and makes the sign of the cross.

Kyrie: Lord have mercy upon us.

Joshua stares at her face. He has never seen such stillness, such heaviness, such impassive leaden weight as in those closed eyes, that set mouth, those rouged cheeks. He imagines her breathing, waits for the rise and fall of her chest, the gentle lifting that would signify breath, life.

He and his wife were the first to venture from Trinidad to Canada. Once settled he planned to bring all five brothers and sisters and finally his parents, even though they complained they were too old to make such a change. None of them realized how lonely it would be. Edmonton, hardly a large cosmopolitan centre, had a fair-sized Arab community but not a large black district. They moved into Sherwood Park, a predominately white Anglo-Saxon bedroom community where they most certainly did not belong. But the rent was cheap. His wife cleaned houses, something he abhorred. She picked up after other people's spoiled children, washed out their bathtub ring, scrubbed greasy pots left soaking in a cold sink because the woman of the house was out working for another TV, a fur coat or a second car.

The two of them sacrificed for the others back home. In this country they lived simply without the amenities they saw others enjoying. But when he felt exhausted, cheated, bitter, Angela cheered him up with a playful poke in the stomach. "C'mon, ole man," she'd say. Though he was not much older than her she teased him because he took his family responsibilities so seriously.

Since Angela was the eldest sister he brought her over first. Nothing broke her spirit. For her it was a great adventure. She adjusted almost too quickly to this alien country. In her graduating year she became a highschool cheerleader and runner up as Queen of the prom and in nurses' training won a scholarship. But to his relief she also held to the old traditions. On Sundays after church the scent of roti filled the house and her hot curry was the best he had tasted since leaving home.

But now as he bends over the coffin he shakes his head at the senseless loss. Why? His wife nudges him to go back to the pew and sit down. The line of her classmates has already formed behind him. They have all come, all the girls and the two young men who graduated with her from nursing.

Dies Irae: Day of wrath and doom impending.

Joshua sat uncomfortably in the plush chair of the Jubilee Auditorium. He still hated suits and ties. But in this cold country, even in summer, one would freeze dressed in a cotton shirt so light that it flapped in the breeze and allowed currents of air to rush up under the armpits. He pulled his camera out of its case and set it on his lap. The pianist struck the first chord of Handel's *Largo* and the audience rose to its feet. There she was, marching down the aisle with the other girls in their starched white uniforms and new white noiseless shoes, cradling an armful of red roses. She stared straight ahead to the stage where the chairs sat in rows waiting. He knew she must be wondering where they were sitting but she dared not look from side to side as they processed down the aisle. She kept in step and smiled as she looked anxiously for her seat. He regretted that in a few more days she would be doing the same thing again, holding flowers and walking down another aisle to another tune and dressed in a white wedding dress. But he could not be there.

When they arrived on stage there was a rustle of white uniforms as the girls found their correct chairs and squeezed beside each other. They waited until everyone was in place and then they sat in one graceful movement. He wondered if she was looking for him now. Their faces wouldn't be so hard to find. She had told him to sit up close so he could take pictures. "I want to send them home," she had said. Her day of glory.

Credo: He was crucified dead and buried and descended into Hell.

The police came right into his office and told him she had already been rushed to emergency. He didn't wait to call his wife or anyone. They asked him questions: the young officer, the medical examiner, even the doctor staring down at his shoes in the Quiet Room.

"Where was she going?"

"To the airport. She was flying to San Francisco."

"Would the family consider donating her cornea? I know it's a hard time for you but..."

"I don't know.... Yes... if it helps somebody else."

"Did you want to make some telephone calls? Would you like a priest? Did you say she had relatives in San Francisco?"

They offered to let him see her before they turned the respirator down but he refused. Then they brought her clothing to him in a brown paper bag. A nurse, crying, slipped the crucifix she had been wearing into his hand. The young policeman drove him home. "Yes. They had the driver of the other car. Bud Fraser. A young kid. Drunk. Yes. He was badly hurt. No. He wasn't dead. Yes. They should raise the driving age. Of course. Bud Fraser would go to court. Yes. A senseless waste. If I can be of any further assistance..."

When he got home he tore up the graduation pictures.

Consecration: When we eat this bread and drink this cup we proclaim your death.

He breathes the heavy odour of burning candles and flowers mixed with the musty smell of the church and feels confused and dizzy as if he has inhaled ether. He concentrates on what her last moments might have been like, hoping that by re-creating the scene in his imagination he will undo the horror of her death, or at least he will fabricate a quick and painless end.

The taxi driver probably got out of the car to help her with the suitcases as she dragged them across the sidewalk. One of them contained her wedding dress. Joshua remembered the day she and his wife had gone shopping. " Seedpearls... sweetheart neckline antique satin... dropped waist." Words he never used, couldn't visualize. But still he knew it was the perfect dress for a San Francisco wedding.

Would she have sat in the front seat to be friendly? The back would have been safer. After she told him, "international airport," she probably would have stopped talking. Instead, she might have rehearsed the name she was soon to enjoy to the click of the metre: Mrs. Greene, Mrs. Sam Greene, Mr. and Mrs. S. Greene. The bride and groom were to fly home to Trinidad immediately after the wedding. She had complained to Joshua that he hadn't used an instant camera so that her mother could see the photos of both special days. A close-up of Angela wearing her nurse's cap, smiling but not too broadly, smiling and gazing into the future, smiling and thinking of the inner-city hospital where she would work. Not for her some smart, sophisticated clinic where all the patients had nose jobs. A formal portrait of Angela in her wedding dress, looking down at her flowers, meditating on them as if they were all that mattered in the world. A picture of Angela and Sam cutting the wedding cake and kissing at the same time, his hand on top of hers guiding the knife. The camera flashes. She blinks. Opening her eyes she is blinded not by the quick sparkle she expected but by an explosion of hard yellow beams that jostle, plunge and thrust at the taxi's window and then with one final lunge break through the glass.

Pastoral Prayer and General Intercession

Events June 20/99

06:00 Anne Bradley, a two year old girl, dies of smoke inhalation when her parent's farm house burns to the ground.

08:00 A helicopter, part of a search and rescue team, crashes in northern Ontario. There are no survivors.

08:30 Bud Fraser undergoes spinal cord surgery.

09:30 A bomb threat closes down the international airport for over an hour.

10:15 Sam Greene flies in from San Francisco.

11:45 The doctor tells Mr. Fraser that Bud is paralyzed from the waist down.

13:30 Angela Armstrong is buried from St. Anthony's Roman Catholic Church.

14:00 Olga Barovsky, Russian gymnast, defects while touring the States.

15:30 Sam Greene flies back to San Francisco.

17:00 A busload of Japanese tourists overturns outside of Mexico City.

Agnus Dei: Lamb of God who takes away the sins of the world, have mercy upon us.

The kneeling bench is hard against his bony knees. At first his foot cramps and then his whole right leg falls asleep. Joshua discreetly sits forward on the edge of the pew and then eases gently into his seat but he miscalculates and falls noisily back into place.

This sudden clumsy lack of control reminds him of the boy. Joshua wanted to kill him. It didn't take long to find out which hospital admitted Bud Fraser. He wanted to stand over him in the bed and threaten him, quietly, so no one would hear, just the kid. Torture wouldn't be good enough. Obeah. Joshua was sure his grandmother would remember. He wished he had brought some of the dirt from Angela's grave to sprinkle on the kid's head. Obeah. The curse.

The nurses came and went like phantoms on rubber soled shoes, only their uniforms rustling when they walked. For a moment he pretended that one of them was Angela. She would have nursed a boy like this, soothed his brow, held his hand, probably given him a rosary or lit a candle for him at mass. One of the nurses scurrying down the hall saw him leaning against the wall.

"Excuse me, Sir. Can I help you?"

"No, thanks," he says and pretends to start moving away.

In the end he doesn't go into the boy's room. He only stands at the doorway, his hands in his pocket, clenching and unclenching his fists. He watches. The angry, well-rehearsed words stick in his throat. His hands relax. He leans against the wall. He has not cried in all this time but now….The kid is sitting up in a wheelchair, staring out the window. He can't be more than sixteen, his arms skinny, resting on the handles, his hands white, frail, fingers long, lifeless. He wears the hospital gown and a baseball cap.

Benediction: Go in the peace of Christ.

The priest breaks the bread and then lifts the host and chalice. The congregation rises and forms a quiet orderly line moving slowly towards him. Joshua's wife is the first to receive. He lets her go before him in deference. The spray of roses trembles as he passes the coffin. He wants to reach out, pick one of them and place it over her crossed hands so that her resting place will smell of at least one flower. If only he had not brought her to this cold country of no spring and short summers, this city fed by a muddy river whose waters, after the endless winter, taste of run-off. He squints his eyes like the quick shutter of the camera, trying to imprint her face forever on some empty blank space in his brain.

He moves away and stands in front of the priest. Cupping his palms together to receive the host, he extends his hands. He hears the priest, "The body of our Lord Jesus Christ, broken for you."

When the mass is ended the priest raises his arms in a final blessing. There is a rustle as the people bow their heads. Then slowly he descends the steps of the sanctuary. Joshua joins the other men at the foot of the coffin and they hoist it on to their shoulders. He stumbles surprised at the weight, and follows the priest solemnly down the aisle past the stained glass window and through the big oak doors into the pale sunlight.

The altar boy genuflects before the crucifix and extinguishes the Paschal candle.

Diva

Angela had an affinity for melancholy. For instance, she preferred Russian composers to French or Italian. The last time we met was under a Vancouver drizzle. The day suited her mood. Even as I joined her at the café and met the new man in her life, she was complaining about something. Was it her agent?

Eric was one of a string of lovers for whom she sought my approval. At least, she used to when we were young.

She and I met in our early twenties in Toronto. I was finishing university and she was at a secretarial school. By coincidence, we studied voice with the same teacher at the Royal Conservatory, the big old gray building on Bloor Street. The first of her many boyfriends was an engineering student. He had clear blue eyes, an intelligent face and a boys'-private-school sophistication. I was quite in love with him myself. In fact, when the affair ended she offered to pass him on to me. But I heard that he was devastated and I was too afraid to compete with her thick black hair and high Italian cheek bones.

Angela laughed at my insecurity. "You've got a great brain. I wish I had your intelligence."

She didn't seem to realize that men easily came under her spell. Even the more temperamental maestros, who were known to purposely drown out singers they didn't like, restrained the whole orchestra when she sang a high note. Instead of competing they embellished her performance, encouraging her to show off trills and grace notes in true *bel canto* style. When she sang, a hush fell over the audience, a moment of stillness descended like the silence at Holy Communion as the wine goblet is raised to the lips.

Eric, her new love, was as infatuated as her audiences. He wouldn't leave us alone together that afternoon, not even for an hour. His presence changed the tone of our meeting from its usual intimacy. We proceeded cautiously, exchanged pleasantries about the city, the number of Japanese tourists, the weather. We only wanted coffee but since there was a cover charge he decided we should have a platter of fruit, though I would have preferred a Caesar salad.

Angela's father had been the same kind of man, the sort who thought he knew what was best and imposed his will. "What's all this talk about music? How much money will you make as a singer? You want to be something practical." Obediently, she began a secretarial course but at my urging applied with me to the opera school. Her documents were forwarded to my house. We were both accepted. In retaliation her father never attended a single concert. "Who do you think you are?" he asked. "What are you trying to prove?"

She became famous for her rather flamboyant version (so the critics said) of Cio-Cio-San, the betrayed young Japanese bride in the opera *Madama Butterfly*. I, on the other hand, played the rather boring role of the maid Suzuki (of whom the critics said nothing.) At the end of the first act when I helped her out of the brocade wedding kimono with the pink lotus flower etched in rhinestones across the back, and Pinkerton clasped her in his arms for the famous love duet, there wasn't a dry eye in the house.

That is how our relationship began and seemed to continue. She sang all the thrilling arias, and held the audience spellbound while I played her foil. Over the years I continued in the supporting roles, helped her exit from bad love affairs gracefully by feeding her clever parting lines, urged her to stand up to her agent when she wasn't making enough money. Perhaps, that was why Eric made me so angry. I was being upstaged.

While studying at the opera school, she won a scholarship to Rome. Now a young and ambitious businessman commanded her destiny.

"Let him wait," I said. "If he really loves you he'll postpone the marriage for a bit. You're throwing away the chance of a lifetime." But in a voice like Eric's, louder than mine, he echoed her insecurity. "You'll never make it. There's far too much competition out there."

"I really love him," she said when we were having one of our intimate coffees together. "I can't make him wait. Anyway, I don't have to stop singing just because I'm married."

Within five years her husband was transferred to Vancouver, he was laid off, she became pregnant and the marriage disintegrated. From then on she worked as a secretary and joined the Vancouver Opera Company chorus to make a little extra money for herself and her son. Now and again she landed a gig at an elegant night club.

As for me, I married an accountant and over the years had five children, all of whom I love dearly. Not one of them even flirted with the arts. Knowing I had little of Angela's charisma, I exchanged the heady spotlights of the theatre for the dim candles of the sanctuary. I became a paid church soloist at Metropolitan United Church where the arts, especially music, were valued as part of the liturgy. Instead of sleeping in on Sundays from late night curtain calls, I went to bed early on Saturday nights. Since the country divided us, we saw each other rarely. When we did, it was I who travelled to Vancouver. "I just don't have the money," she would complain. Each meeting took off from the last as if it happened only yesterday. We embraced like delighted school girls, shared secrets, made confessions, healed and encouraged each other until my next visit.

The last time I called, she seemed as eager as ever to see me.

"I need a holiday," I said. "Things aren't going well at home."

"That husband of yours being a bad boy again? After twenty years you must be used to him by now."

"I need a dose of cheering up."

But when I called the second time to confirm our plans, she was distant. "I don't think I'll be in the city. You see, I have this new man in my life, Eric. We may go fishing for the long weekend."

"Why didn't you tell me before I booked my flight?" I slammed the phone into the cradle and then called my travel agent to cancel the ticket, but it was too late. The next night I phoned her again. "Look, I can't change my plans. I'm coming to Vancouver whether or not you're there. Could I sleep at your place?" The request seemed so natural. We had so often put each other up in sleeping bags or on chesterfields over the years.

"No, my son is having friends over. We really don't have the room."

"C'mon Angela. What happened to the fishing trip?"

"Well, actually it's cancelled. We had a fight and I haven't heard from him. I hope he'll phone me tonight. What I mean is, I want to leave the weekend free in case he calls or comes over or maybe I'll...."

"Forget it, I'll call you in Vancouver."

When I arrived I resisted phoning her and went for a walk in a persistent drizzle around English Bay. But the ocean brought back memories of our last meeting and her urgent need to be admired. Strolling along the beach that day she had patted her stomach and said, "I'm still getting the *ingenue* roles. Do I look young enough?"

She drove herself jogging, weight-lifting, bicycling, trying to keep her figure youthful and trim. She complained bitterly she did not have enough money for a face lift. Meanwhile, I aged, I hoped somewhat gracefully. At each first encounter I could feel her sizing me up. Then, she would tell me about a new diet she had discovered or a rare wrinkle cream. "You really must try it. It's done wonders for me. Do you notice?"

During that visit I saw a video of her most recent concert. She and a young tenor were hired to entertain on a cruise ship bound for Alaska. They put together a program of Puccini, featured *Madama Butterfly* and added a touch of the dying Mimi from *La Bohème*. As an encore the two of them grandly performed the love duet from the last act of *La Traviata*, just before Violetta dies of consumption. Angela was still at her best in melancholia. For the first time I noticed the intense effort, the strain on her voice.

"Could you take a break between arias? Rest your voice? Get a glass of water?" I had suggested tactfully.

"No. There's no backstage. Why? You could tell I was getting tired?"

"Oh no, you sound wonderful. Marvellous concert."

At the time, I thought her lack of energy was simply a symptom of approaching middle age, a reality that haunted us both. I complimented her, appealing to the narcissism that I had tolerated with amusement over the years.

This time, as I strolled by the slate-coloured ocean, I couldn't get her out of my mind. For me she would always be the little Cio-Cio-San straining for the perfect high C, waiting for the errant lover, the passionate embrace, the standing ovation. I went back to the hotel room and phoned.

"Hi, it's me. Are you free? My plane got in late last night."

"Great. How about this afternoon around three?"

"Not 'til then? Sure."

"I'm so sorry we haven't much time. We're going out for dinner."

"You and Eric made up, huh?"

"Yes. I'll bring him along. You'll love him."

"Can't we just visit, the two of us? I've got so much to tell you."

"I can't leave him sitting alone all afternoon! We'll see you at three."

When we finished our platter of strawberries I let overweight, overbearing Eric pay the bill. "We need a few moments alone together," I said.

"We're going to meet friends," he said.

"I've come a long way to see you," I turned to Angela.

"Five minutes," he said looking at his watch and strode off importantly.

I wanted to tell her about the struggles in my marriage, the new career plans I was slowly devising. I wanted her spirited encouragement. Instead we argued.

"What's with you? This man's ordering you around? He's just like your dad. Your husband was the same. Haven't you learned anything yet? " I asked.

"I told you not to come. I said I was busy. Eric's special."

"So am I. I'm your oldest friend," I said. She made a lame apology of sorts, called me Dear and Love, names she never used before.

"I'll phone you tonight," she said.

That evening, after a cheap dinner, I picked my way through the puddles back to the Sylvia Hotel. My bathroom plumbing had a leak and the constant drip was annoying. The romance and history of the place no longer pleased me but felt worn and jaded. I waited for the promised phone call, the apology no matter how brief, the offer to come to Toronto soon. But my only comfort was a big picture window that overlooked the sea. I knelt down and gazing into the wet night remembered the many times the two of us had taken the same position on stage. In my mind I could hear strains of the Waiting Song as Madama Butterfly and her maid watch the American ship glide into the harbour. But this time there was no dear friend beside me and I wanted to weep. Instead, I leapt to my feet, shut the drapes and turned out the lights. I went to bed and let the stars fall into oblivion and the sun rise on its own.

I was too hurt and angry to contact Angela again. She didn't call me, either. I figured she and Eric must have married, and as so often happens with women, she dropped her old friends and centered her life around him. Then, about five years later, I heard news of her through an old acquaintance. By that time I had divorced my husband and graduated from a community college that offered a diploma in Administration and the Arts. It's too late to be a performer but I can still belong to the artists' community and make a contribution, I thought. I was hired by a small theatre to do promotional work, and prided myself in giving some young musicians their first break.

That was when Madame Vinci came blustering into my office. In her youth she was an old rival of Angela's but lacked her dramatic quality. Now, in her middle age, she was one of Toronto's leading vocal coaches. She wanted me to arrange a concert for one of her former students who was finishing up a tour of the western provinces.

"Too bad about Angela," she said as her dyed red curls bobbed garishly.

"What happened?"

"Haven't you heard?" She waited for me to confess my ignorance. "Cancer of the throat. She's been fighting it for years. Started with the breast. I'm surprised you didn't know. You two were so close."

"I had no idea. I thought she was happily married. There was a man, Eric…"

"Angela never had any luck with men. Now this!" Madame Vinci flounced out of the room.

When I arrived at the hospital she was already in a coma. The room was bare and even more ugly than the operatic chamber where so many times before she had sung her farewell. Her distracted son wept openly as we embraced.

"You're exhausted. You need rest. Why don't you let me sit with her tonight?"

When I took her hand, I thought she responded. The nurse came into the room and said, "It's okay to talk to her. Hearing is the last to go."

I wanted to stay until she died but my obligations at home were pressing. I spent three days at her bedside, trying to make up for the years of silence and reproach, caring for her with the same devotion I had portrayed so many times on stage.

On the last day I came to the ward with a Walkman. The nurse helped me put the ear phones gently in her ears and adjust the volume so that she could hear in her last moments the strains of *Madama Butterfly*. I stayed with her all that night as the moon lit up the ships in the Vancouver harbour and the sun cast a pale yellow light over the horizon.

New York, New York,

i. Spaces

On my days off I wandered about the museums and art galleries of Manhattan. I liked the Frick Collection the best. There was something familiar and inviting about the old building that had once been a private residence and now was the home of an assortment of art works beloved by one man.

The place was just what it said, a collection. There seemed to be no order, just a conglomeration of art works placed randomly about the house. I gave up trying to follow the guidebook, just as I had despaired of maps when I tried to find my way about the city. By the time I left the Collection, I wasn't sure I had visited every room. No one century was represented on a wall. No one country. Show cases of sculptures, small bronzes, and porcelains were situated side by side. Eighteenth century French furniture stood stolidly on oriental rugs. Drawings by Gainsborough and Gauguin hung in the same room. I could admire the delicate luminescence of Monet's paintings and then quickly shift my eyes to the dark shadows of Toulouse-Lautrec.

I stopped by a painting called *Vetheuil in Winter* by Monet. The cold grays and blues crept off the canvas and enveloped my shoulders. I shivered and wrapped my arms around myself. But when I entered the next room, I was transfixed by Turner's painting, *The Harbor of Dieppe*. I felt bathed in the gold and crimson colors. In time, I came to like the fact that there seemed to be no rhyme nor reason to the displays.

When I meandered into the last room of my journey, I looked out the window at what was supposed to be a beautiful garden. It was under construction. I sat on a bench and watched the workmen as they replaced the stone wall and fixed the wrought iron fence. I couldn't imagine what it would be like when it was finished. Where the flowering bushes would grow or the fountain, if there was one, would be placed. But I believed that eventually it would be beautiful.

ii. Cuckoo

I think my favorite show on Broadway was *One Flew Over the Cuckoo's Nest* because it reminded me of where I work, Gethsemane Hospice. We are all mad here, too. I am a chaplain, not for the mentally ill but for the dying. However, the issues are the same. For instance, in the play the patients have voluntarily committed themselves for treatment. The insane want to get well, live a wholesome and meaningful existence. Here, at Gethsemane, the dying also admit themselves into the hospice. They know they are making a transition into a new life and they want help as they "pass over."

So, we have therapy and group meetings, just like they do in the play. We have support groups, groups to talk about cancer, pain control and bereavement. We have Christmas concerts, and birthday celebrations, live bands, balloons and iced cake with candles. In the play, the nurses communicate with the patients behind a glass wall and with a microphone so that their disembodied voices bounce off the walls and fill the ward. At Gethsemane we have pages you can hear even in the washrooms and fire exits:

Dr. Jerome 2113
Pastoral Care 2341
Code blue, fourth floor
The patient support group is about to begin in the conference room.
And we have our Miss Ratched.

The Director of our department smiles, just like the nurse in the play, a wide smile, though she never shows her teeth, when she says, "No." The difference is, she disciplines staff, not patients—she has no power over the sick. But she does oppress us. Three negative reports mailed off to Human Resources and you're out. Her words cut like sharp scissors, ripping a garment up the seams leaving it frayed and formless. I saw the Hispanic chaplain leave her office crying. The Afro-American minister refuses to eat lunch with us in the cafeteria. She takes a tray up to her office, a windowless cubicle, and sits at her computer where she munches on a sandwich. "I'm just keepin' to myself," she told me. "Too many eyes watchin'." (The secretary times our coffee and lunch breaks and reports any infraction to the director. Our Miss Ratched has other spies, too. The worst insult among the staff is to be accused of being an informer.)

It's a control issue, just like in the play. In one scene, the patients want to watch the world series on TV. Miss Ratched refuses their request. "It's not on the schedule, not part of the tradition," she patiently explains. You would think she would want them to have some fun, that it would be part of their therapy.

Our director is the same. She wants to make sure I know she's boss so she criticizes me for consorting too much with the staff, causing too much laughter, not communicating, allowing our students too many coffee breaks. All that criticism said in a gentle voice, while smiling.

We pray every morning, the nun, the priest, the two Protestant ministers and the ex-priest who still works in the department by a letter of permission from the bishop. What good do our prayers do? Keep away the evil spirits? Give us courage as we go upstairs to hold thin hands and gaze at gaunt faces? When our Miss Ratched joins us, we stay glued to our seats, even if the morning worship is finished. No one wants to lock eyes with her or show an independent spirit which might be interpreted as disrespect. Each one of us is dependent upon her in some way. I'm here on a religious visa, waiting for my green card. Until the paper work is finished, I can't get a position in another hospital. Two of the chaplains are students and the other three are hoping to get certified, the official stamp of approval from the professional organization.

Fear is what dominates our department. Not fear of God. Not fear of death. Fear of a bad evaluation. Fear of a non-compliance record filed in Human Resources. Fear of a security guard stepping into one of our offices and saying, "You have an hour to gather up your things." Fear of our Miss Ratched and her smile.

iii. Right To Life

Brother John was doing his field work in our hospital. One day he took me to a Vietnamese restaurant. To get there, we had to walk through the Bowery to the edge of Chinatown. So he acted as my guide and, whistled bluegrass gospel songs as we trudged through the summer heat. I've been to Greenwich Village and Soho, the Upper East Side, the West Side, Harlem, even Hell's Kitchen but I'd forgotten all about the Bowery. Who'd want to remember it? Except for a certain seedy glamour? The Bowery Boys. Stephen Foster who nearly died there, alone and destitute.

We passed the projects where Brother John worked the first year he was in seminary. After mass, he visited the sick, shut-ins, and young mothers whose children were in his confirmation class. "I wore my habit on the streets. You'd be surprised the stories people tell if you just sit down for a spell and talk," he said.

We passed vegetable stands where they sell Chinese cabbage, tofu and bean sprouts. Metal panels painted with graffiti. Bars Brother John used to frequent. We passed the Soup Kitchen the Salvation Army runs. "Want to go in?" he asked. We passed a newsstand with its gruesome headline about a drunk cop. A pawn shop, its windows aglitter with watches and gold earrings.

Brother John is an activist and thinks he'll probably end up in prison one day fighting for the rights of the unborn. "There's no place more dangerous for a baby than a mother's womb," he says. Should he be incarcerated for a long period of time, say three years, he intends to practice prayer and contemplation and grow closer to God.

If I worked in one of those bars he used to visit, and should I get pregnant at nineteen, I wonder, would I go to a one of those clinics and get an abortion? If not, I suppose I'd raise my kid in the Bowery, collect welfare and hope my boyfriend would be like a dad to my baby, even if he wasn't her father.

I guess Brother John would like that.

iv. Reb Abe's Departure

For the blessing and not for the curse. For plenty and not for scarcity. For life and not for death —Pirkei Avot 2:16,15

Abe wore bright colours, turquoise or blue ties, a yarmulke to match. But expensive shoes were his favorite. He said he had a foot fetish.

On his last day, everyone came to the party, not just the nurses and doctors but techs, cleaning staff, and security guards. Father Godfrey took pictures. The one of Abe cutting the cake is tacked up on the bulletin board in my office.

We worked the evening shift on Sundays. Between the hospital pages, when someone died or went on the critical list, we ate Chinese food ordered in from the local restaurant. Abe always paid and insisted I take the left-overs home. So, I tasted ginger and soya sauce half way into the next week.

At the commemoration of Kristallnacht, he invited me to light a candle at the service in the chapel. I shared the Passover meal with him and a few patients, when he blessed the bitter and the sweet. We ate nuts and raisins in the sukkah. He took me out to the patio on the day it was constructed and explained how the little hut, covered in vine leaves, represented the tent the ancient Hebrews set up and took down on their journey through the desert. I watched when the dwelling was dismantled and dragged away. The space was always empty after that, even though a potted plant stood in its place. When the choir came to celebrate Purim, he taught me the song:

O tanasteli shalom aleichem
Heim sh'ru: B'ruchim habaim shalom aleichem.
Just another foreigner in another foreign land
But I knew he was my brother when he took me by the hand.

v. Dead-Eye Dick

Father Godfrey is a Pranic Healer, moves energies in the tradition of ancient Hindus, blesses departing souls as they rise, scans tumors and rashes which disappear, reads Tarot cards.

One morning, the express stalled between Manhattan and the Bronx. Two hours late for work and mass, stranded on a bridge, high above sky scrapers, he loosened his clerical collar. Drawn by the sunshine, he wandered through the train, out a sliding door and cautiously balanced his two feet on the ledge between cars. Then, overcome by an urgent need, peed. The yellow stream sprayed concrete buttresses, wings of a pigeon, tops of cars, but not a drop on his shoes.

Business men, lap top computers, poised on their knees, noticed. "They call me Dead-Eye Dick," laughed Father Godfrey.

vi. Lung Cancer

"I want to die." Louie sat upright in bed. Supported himself on a horizontal bar. Pulled on it with thin arms. Straightened his back. Sputtered and gasped.

"He's going to die," whispered the nurse as she fixed the IV tubes. "He's having an anxiety attack. Can you stay and hold his hand?"

"I won't leave you," I said. "Breathe deeply." The whites of his eyes showed, his hand a claw in mine.

I sat with him all morning. The doctor wrote in his chart while Louie heaved and sighed.

At last his wife came. "The car broke down," she said. "I would have been here earlier." She took my place and his hand.

"This is a hard time for you," I said.

"God is good," she answered. "The mechanic fixed the car right away when I told him about my husband. God is good," she said. "We had a great life together. Ten years. I was married before. He's my second husband. So sweet to me." She kissed and stroked his hand.

The doctor finally came with morphine and Louie slept and breathed. The next day he and his wife played cards at the bedside table.

"I still want to die," he said, holding the joker in his hand. "I was ready."

"God is good," said his wife. "We have another day."

A week later, Louie was labeled, chronically depressed.

"Just let me die," he said. "I was ready." The nurse gave him ativan, a relaxant.

Then God was good. It happened three weeks later.

vii. Museum Curator

We tasted miso soup, eels, and seaweed, rolling each morsel in our mouths, savoring the salty taste. Our evening in Soho was presented on a wooden platter and then dished to blue ceramic plates—pink shrimp, shredded white radishes, raw crimson tuna and greens. I thanked my dead father for taking the family to Lichee Gardens in Toronto's Chinatown, where I learned to use chopsticks. I didn't drop a single bit of soya sauce or noodle on the orchid dress I chose to wear that night to match my mauve nail polish. I had no purple shoes.

When I looked into Ned's violet eye (he wore a black patch over the other one) my tongue became a dry twig lodged in my cavernous mouth.

At the next table, separated only by the hanging corners of our white tablecloths, sat two women. One of them was opening a box, pulling out paper, a present carefully wrapped.

"What a beautiful lantern," Ned said to her. He pointed to the ceiling. The same collapsible lamps illuminated the restaurant.

"I'm hanging it in the gallery," she said. "At my opening."

I couldn't place her accent.

The artist's sake was contained in a square wooden box, resting in a ceramic bowl. When the waiter had poured it out, the wine overflowed into the second container. I wondered how the woman would drink from there without spilling it down her chin.

They chatted on, while my sapling tongue wrapped itself around food not words. Later, when she had gone to the ladies room, he said that her sculptures were being shown at a famous gallery. "She's made it," he said.

Then I won him back with questions.

"Where did you learn about art?" I asked him. He told me how he tried to escape to Canada during the Vietnam War but was conscripted. However, he didn't get sent over because his brother was already there. Instead, he learned how to make wood sculptures on the army base in Texas. As he stared at the tissue paper strewn on the artist's table, he described the special wooden crates he built and how he packed artifacts collected in Osaka and Yokohama, so they would arrive unbroken in New York museums. He had spent thousands.

I asked why he lived all the way out on Long Island when he loved Soho so much and he told me about a lover who had enticed him to buy a house on the ocean.

"Tell me about yourself," he said.

"My life is boring in comparison to yours," I said.

So, I told him about my first husband, and the divorce and my second husband and his strokes and my two children and a bit about why I came to New York.

Then my tongue became a log like the one in someone's eye in the New Testament. I looked down at my gleamy plate and began to eat greens that resembled big snow peas.

"Don't bite them," he said laughing.

Then he showed me how to suck the smooth sweet seeds out of the salty pod.

viii. Matriarch

I took the free tour when I visited the American Museum of Natural History. As we walked from the lobby to the first exhibit, the young guide told me that she wanted to be a cultural anthropologist but continued study was much too expensive. So, she got married, works on Wall Street but volunteers at the museum and therefore stays close to her passion. Her diamond ring glittered in the darkness. She held up a blue flag so none of us would lose her in the crowd and we dutifully fell in behind.

We arrived at the scene where we could view the gorillas. "This animal is an endangered species because its habitat is becoming limited," she said. I stared at the scene. The creatures looked real against the pale blue sky and trees. The male stood on his hind legs pounding his chest. "He's scaring off the intruder you can see in the corner. This is his pride," she said. "Actually, for all their size, gorillas are very gentle. Now should you be lost in the jungle one day," she giggled, "and you meet a gorilla, don't run. Pick up a twig and start chewing. Don't look him in the eye and just back off. He won't bother you." The female, munching on a leaf, sat in the tall grass with her baby, looking safe and content. I would like to have walked through the protective glass and joined them, lolled in the meadow and let him protect me.

I too am becoming extinct, I thought. My habitat is being destroyed. I am an older single woman and I no longer fit into society. The environs belong to nubile young women and muscular men. Everyone is in couples or with children. I am wandering through New York City without a mate, tribe or herd. I eat in restaurants alone, go home on the express bus before it gets too dark, hope for a message on my answering machine but when I check it, there is no flashing green light. Like the gorillas, my days are numbered.

Then, she took us to the Imax film and we watched a documentary about sea otters. The narrator admonished us, who were city dwellers, to value fresh water and not waste it. He reminded the audience that all creatures are interdependent. He told us how the sea otter was nearly killed off for its fur, and how the subaqueous community was dying because these animals were nearly extinct. If it weren't for some conservationists, the sea otters would have disappeared and with them the teeming world that lives under the waves. I watched the playful creatures cavort in the water unaware of how precarious was their own life. The camera dove under the surface and showed us the newly growing sea weed, and little fish that were replenished because of the increasing number of sea otters. I wondered what would be lost if I died or what would be gained if I lived. Very little, I thought.

Then our Wall Street guide took us to the last exhibit, and drew our attention to a large herd of elephants towering above us in the middle of the hall. She pointed out how the babies link trunks with their mothers so they don't get lost or trampled. When they have reached maturity, the young males go off on their own to mate. So, the group consists mainly of mothers and babies. But heading the herd is the oldest and wisest female. She stands out front, head held high, white tusks flashing, ears back, ready to charge.

ix. Terrace Gala

The City Club of St. Bartholomew's Church held its annual dinner dance on the terrace at the end of June. A storm had been predicted, but, so far, the weather report was wrong. It gave me something to talk about, though. During a lull in the conversation I could say to a new acquaintance, "Hmm, I wonder if it will rain."

"Looks like it. Well, they're all set up if we have to dash inside."

"Oh that's good. Of course, we could huddle under the umbrellas," I might add.

Laughter.

Over each table a jaunty red or yellow umbrella swayed. A couple of candles and flowers added to the festive mood. Tiny white lights circled the green branches of potted trees. The band played too loudly for us to engage in conversation. Some couples were already dancing. I took a picture but the flash didn't work.

The seating was pre-assigned by a small number on the left hand corner of the name tags. I put my umbrella down on the chair at table number eleven and then maneuvered my way to the bar and bought a glass of white wine. I mingled. Groups of old friends gathered in tight circles. The City Club was for singles over forty. Some of the members had been coming for years. "It's not a match making place, a meat market. It's just a place to have fun together," a bearded man said on the first night I attended.

"I'm hoping to make some friends. I'm new here. Just moved."

"Where from?"

"Canada, Alberta."

"Been to Montreal. It's a pretty city. Well, welcome to Manhattan. Lots to see here. You should go to the Frick." He moved on before I could say that I'd already been there, and I was living in the Bronx.

On the first Friday of the month, wine and hors d'oeuvres were served on a terrace that overlooked the city. That's where I met Hugo. He had fine sensitive hands with long tapering fingers. He could have been a piano player or an artist.

When he took my number he said, "We people from the Bronx have to stick together."

He phoned me every Wednesday and we went out five Saturdays evenings, for dinner and a movie, or a gallery. I knew he wasn't my type but he gave me companionship, a sense of security, safety. "Have a good week," he would say in a kindly tone. He kept his distance, though. No holding hands in the movie. A peck on the cheek when we met or said good night at the bus stop. Then, I went home to Alberta for a visit and when I returned to New York the phone calls stopped, except for the remainder the week before the Terrace Gala.

I chatted with a rather large thirtyish woman in a pink cotton dress, and then a man who worked in the Chase Manhattan post office. I noticed Hugo in one of the intimate circles of friends. He must have seen me, I thought. Why hasn't he spoken? I went over to him and he introduced me to his friends, a woman in a red beaded jacket and a very thin man in blue jeans and a cashmere blue sweater. Then Hugo sauntered away. I stared at the empty space he had left, now filled with the gray stone wall of the church. To my relief, someone announced at the microphone that dinner would be served.

Two married couples were seated at my table. They had met at the club. The third couple lived together. Bill, the man beside me with the girlfriend on his left, was an investment counselor. That provided conversation for the dinner which followed. I told him that I had five thousand dollars in a savings account and he gave me his card. We finished the grilled chicken, which we agreed was too dry. The second bottle of wine came too late for the first course, but we drank it anyway along with the chocolate mousse.

When the dancing began, I was left at the table alone, so I went to the Ladies Room, checked my hair in the mirror and applied some lipstick. I avoided Hugo's table but then on the way back, I forgot where he was sitting and passed right by him. "The next dance is ours," he said. But when the band started up an old Elvis Presley hit, he didn't appear. When Bill came back he pulled out his girlfriend's chair and she sat down. The M.C. announced a Paul Jones. I wanted to get up and leave, take the express bus back to the Bronx. I had a flashback to high school gym classes and dancing lessons.

"C'mon," said Bill. "I won't take no for an answer."

I joined the inner circle of women and when the music stopped, Hugo was in front of me. He danced sedately, carefully. His arm so light around me, I could hardly feel it.

"I tried to leave a message on your answering machine this morning. I think it's out of tape," he said.

"Oh. I didn't know you had called. That was nice of you."

"Just wanted to remind you about tonight."

When the music ended and the circles were formed, I ended up without a partner. Back at table eleven, I checked the bus schedule but the last one had just left. I watched the dancers and remembered how my second husband, Bob, liked to "trip the light fantastic" as he used to say, before the stroke happened and he went into the nursing home. When the couples returned Bill's girlfriend was admiring the dress of one of the married women. "It's my wedding dress," she said. "I haven't worn it for a couple of years. Figured it was time to take it out of the closet."

"It's beautiful," said her companion. She wore a white satin jacket with rhinestone buttons and a chiffon skirt.

I didn't think so. Not half as chic as mine when I married Bob five years ago, I thought.

"My wedding dress was turquoise, crushed silk, with a flounce at the hem," I wanted to say. "Bought it in Savannah, Georgia when Bob took me to meet his family. Still fits, too." But I didn't interject.

Bill asked me to dance. "What would I do without you tonight?" I said, laughing. His warm hand pressed the small of my back. We took long sweeping steps and then two small ones, our hips swaying in rhythm. He was easy to follow. I could have leaned against him. When we returned to the table, he stood behind his girlfriend's chair and ran his fingers up and down her arm. She paid no attention and kept talking to the woman in the wedding dress. They were discussing real estate, now. Still his hands lingered on her shoulders, her elbows. I shivered. "C'mon, Sweetheart. Let's dance," he said. The others followed. I looked over my shoulder and saw that Hugo's place was vacant. He was dancing too.

I pushed my chair back and ran down the stone steps to the sidewalk in order to hail a yellow cab, but none of the drivers would take me back to the Bronx. Panic. What to do? Eventually, I spied a hotel doorman and tipped him to get me a taxi. The driver was from Pakistan. As we sped down the freeway, he told me he had been in New York for fourteen years.

"How do you like it?" I asked.

"Hate it," he said. "Too big. Too violent. Too lonely."

"I've just moved, here. It's quite an adjustment."

"Getting married in five months, though. My parents chose her," he continued.

"An arranged marriage?"

"Yes. Always said that would never happen to me. But when I lost my business, my girlfriend walked out. So, I told my parents to find me a bride. Then we'll move to Hamilton, Ontario," he said. "It's so clean."

"Hamilton? My daughter lives there. I'm Canadian." I screamed in delight.

Jazz Man

I called her as soon as I had unpacked my bags. She was cold and diffident, not like her old self, not like the Myra who used to sit drinking wine, unfolding her story, little by little.

When I first met her and took her to the Red Lion, she was painfully shy, clutching her purse all the way as we drove down Jarvis Street. The only daughter of one of Toronto's old aristocratic families, she knew the lounge's history, a skid-row hang out for pimps and drug pushers. Recently, new owners renovated and transformed the old building into an intimate and rather exclusive jazz club. For me it was refuge where we could listen to the music and talk between sets, a warm and quiet place caught standing upright between the crossfire of two impersonal modern downtown streets.

Who knows what had made her so frightened of the real world? As a young girl she had been enrolled by her parents in a rather religious private girls' school, St. Clement's. Immediately after graduation, she met her husband, a distant, hard-driving law student whom she had met through a girlfriend whose brother went to Upper Canada College. Delighted with the match, her parents gave her a baby grand piano as a wedding present. Above it she hung the ARCT certificate from the Royal Conservatory of Music. Apparently, she harboured a secret dream of becoming a concert artist. But instead of playing at the Roy Thomson Hall, she gave piano lessons to children in order to help her husband through law school.

As for the marriage, it must have been for her as cold and passionless as the mechanical ticking of the metronome, that imposes order but no passion, no joy. Even the pregnancy she longed for was unwanted by him. "Give me a chance to breathe," he said. "I'm just getting started in my career." A few months later, after their little girl was born, he drew up a generous separation agreement. But for Myra, his brisk exit meant the beginning of untold fear and despair. That's why I took her to the Red Lion. I thought she could use a night out. "I don't know much about progressive jazz," she said. The discordant chords floated in the stale thick air.

"Just let it soak in. It'll grow on you."

Trained in the classical style, she watched and listened to the combo like a newly converted Catholic unused to, but fascinated by, the mass.

I noticed a change in her after she met Barth, the black fellow who sat at our table one night because of the crowd. Oh, she confessed to me later and wanted penance and forgiveness but I knew what it was like to be lonely.

"How could I take him home to my family?" she said. "What would I do with him at Christmas?"

We met him the night Big Miller sang blues. This fellow, not a man in a nice gray three-piece suit, mind you, but a person glorious with colour, dressed in a gold casual sweater and russet jacket, sat down right beside her.

"Mind if I join you? Name's Barth." She moved her chair a little to make room for him, as I poured wine into both their glasses. "Where's Norm Amadio? He's supposed to be playing tonight."

"He's in California," she said. "He's accompanying Anne Murray."

"I came all the way to see him."

And so they began speaking. I think she found herself telling him things she had only shared with me.

"Hey, man, life is full of ups and downs. Once, I wanted to be a pilot in the Canadian Air Force but in those days they wouldn't let a black man fly a plane."

"I always wanted to be a blues singer," she said. "But I studied classical music, instead." She sang for him softly while he clicked his fingers, beating out the syncopated jazz rhythm so different from what she had learned at the Royal Conservatory.

"Love me or leave me and let me be lonely," she crooned.

"You should get up and sing with the group," Barth said. "There's not too many people here tonight, they'd let you." He took both hands to pull her out of the chair.

"No, I wouldn't dare. I might make a fool of myself," she said.

"Not at all," he said. His fingers still lightly touched hers.

That was how they first met. She told me they ran into each other again, quite by accident, at a Saturday afternoon jazz concert. This time she was with a younger woman who was really looking for a date. When her friend ditched her for a sporting young man with a mustache, Barth asked her out for a beer. He seemed like an old friend as they chatted about music. He invited her out for dinner. At first, she resisted.

"Come with me," he said. "You need something to eat, by now."

Myra heard her voice, scarcely above a whisper, shyly assenting. She floated out the door, his hand on her shoulder guiding her into the street. During dinner he told her more about himself.

"I still work for the Air Force but in the lab. We experiment on animals. Ever hear about people getting the bends when they dive?"

"Yes."

"Same thing happens in space. We simulate it and watch the reactions, rise in blood pressure and so forth."

"Poor monkey," she said.

"Dogs. We use dogs. Sounds awful, eh? Yeah, man, never became a pilot. Never got the promotion I wanted, either."

"Do you hate white people?" she said.

"Once, yes I did. But you learn to forgive."

They finished dinner and went to his car.

"I want to dance with you and hold you close," he said.

They went to a quiet place where the music was slow, then she let him take her home. "My own car was in the underground garage but I didn't even mention it. I couldn't break free from him," she told me later. "What am I doing, alone in my house with this strange man? I thought. But he talked to me and held me for the longest time before we made love. I had forgotten what tenderness was."

Before he left they showered together and stood motionless under the spray, their bodies gleaming. They must have looked like two stones, black and white, that children take home from the beach, polish and treasure.

That night she slept peacefully and in the morning awoke smiling, believing he was still there. When she saw the empty white pillow in the antiseptic light of the morning, surprise and guilt came over her. "I made love to a middle-aged black man who picked me up like a common tramp at a bar."

"He seemed like a kind man," I said and turned away and listened to the music. I suppose I should have understood that she was frightened of him, his freedom, his passion, his jazz, his black world and all that it represented. She wanted me to protect her, keep her safe within the boundaries she knew. But I loved her too much to do that.

She didn't call me for weeks. I heard she had series tickets for the Bach festival at the Roy Thomson hall. On the Easter holidays, I went to the Barbados on a jazz cruise that featured Norm Amadio and his band. When I got home, I decided to call her again.

"Hi, how's it going?"

"All right."

"I just got back from the Barbados."

"Really?"

"Yeah, I was on a jazz cruise."

"Sound like you had a good time."

"I did. C'mon down to the Red Lion and I'll show you my pictures."

I watched her walk into the dimly lit room. It took her a moment to remember where we used to sit and then she saw me. In spite of herself, she smiled and we embraced.

"Long time, no see," I said. Then I told her about my trip.

"They'll be calling you a groupie soon," she said.

"Come with me next time. It's great fun."

"I've given up the whole jazz scene," she said.

"But you love it. You always wanted to sing the blues. Listen."

The flutist's arpeggio coiled upward like the rings of cigarette smoke. Then suddenly, the musicians burst into a frenzy of their own minor chords. But the steady rhythm of the bass anchored the runaway melodies. They fed off each other's energy, building on different modulations and tunes.

When the set was over, the bass player came off the platform and sat beside me.

"So, you got over the cruise," he said.

"You're great tonight," I said. "Right on."

"As always. Whose this?"

I introduced Myra. "She's got a secret love for jazz." Turning to her, I said, "You almost sang here one night. Remember? Barth thought you had a great voice. Love me or leave me. Wasn't that your number?"

"Yes," she said with the old shyness returning.

"Well, there's not too many people here if you want to try," he said. "What's your key?"

"D minor."

Then I watched her follow him to the front of the room. She seemed led by him, propelled by him, as she had felt hypnotized by Barth the night he took her home. But it wasn't the black man who seduced her, nor the artist who led her to the piano. Some other person deep inside her being called out for recognition, for escape, a stranger whom she half knew, half feared. A creature who was strong and sensuous and beautiful.

She held the mike in her hand and followed the rhythms of the bass. She heard a voice, the stranger's, warm and husky like red wine. But it was her voice, Myra's voice that filled the room. She stood a little apart from the other musicians, alone, tall and straight, like a priestess chanting incantations.

Saved

Almus means *to nourish* in Latin. Almus Harvey was a Presbyterian minister from a prominent New England family. His father, a senator, cut him off financially when his son chose the church over politics. His wife was a kindergarten teacher and they had a five year old boy. I learned all that the first night in Princeton, the summer we tried the qualifying exams for the doctorate.

My thesis, *Religious Faith As A Coping Mechanism In Terminal Patients*, allowed me to explore Kübler Ross' theory that faith was a resource for people in suffering and even death. For five years I worked as an intensive care nurse on what I call the front lines, in the emergency and the cardiac and burn units. But it was the cancer patients in palliative care that finally got to me. I remember Allan, who begged God to take him. "Let me go," he moaned, gasping for breath until the doctor wrote the order for more morphine. There was the little boy with legs like toothpicks who whispered, while his dad lifted him out of bed and carried him to the toilet, "I wish they'd just let me go to Jesus." And then, the painter, a Vietnam war veteran, who went into spasms before he died. Unable to speak, he lay on his back with his hands curled like a dog's paws. At our last conversation he nodded at the crucifix, and said to me, "My life was a walk in the park, compared to His."

When I met these patients, I kept thinking about the story of Job, and how God let the Devil test him. I marveled that, like the Hebrew patriarch, they maintained their faith. Finally, I took a leave of absence and went back to school. There were twelve of us that summer, two women and nine men. The other woman dropped out half way through. The men were all married. I, newly divorced.

There was no air conditioning in the class rooms. Small desks. Hard seats. The yellow chalk made a soft caressing sound on the green board. Most of the time, I sat as far away from Almus as possible. Discreet. My first paper was based on the Carl Jung's book, *Answer to Job*. What fascinated me was his statement, "Evil is in the heart of God."

"You find God in the lived experience," said the professor. "Whether good or bad. It's the relationship that sustains and finally heals."

"He should get out from behind his books and live my experience," I said to Almus. We had just left the seminar and my presentation hadn't gone over very well. The professor said I sounded like a Zoroastrian, someone who believes that a cosmic battle between good and evil is being waged in the universe. "Do you know much about Zoroastrianism?" I asked.

"It's an ancient monotheistic religion that emerged out of Persia, long before Judaism. You should go to the library and read up on it," said Almus.

"Maybe that's what I do believe." We were sitting on a park bench and I was close to tears.

"Sounds like you're angry." he said. "You've got a right to be."

"I'm worn out," I said. "I've met Job too many times."

"When you think about it, no matter what happened to him, he never lost his faith in the goodness of God," said Almus. "Sure he asked questions. We all do. But remember what Job finally said?"

"I haven't a clue."

"I know that my Redeemer lives."

"Handel's *Messiah*." I thought for a moment and then countered. "I go along with what Jung wrote. God and the Devil play a cat and mouse game with poor Job."

"Don't be so morose," he said laughing and pulling me to him.

That was the first time he put his arms around me. I leaned into him but he pushed me gently away. However, his hands remained just above my waist at the rib cage. I could feel their heat through my clothes. He held me apart from his body. A decorous space between us. "You should have stuck up for yourself," he said. "You have a lot to say. You're too shy."

"I suppose so," I said.

The next day we went jogging in the park. I couldn't keep up. We slowed down to a walk. I was embarrassed that I wasn't more athletic and made a crack about what? His muscles? I didn't mean it as a come-on. Beads of sweat on his forehead. His strong mouth open, laughing. The green grass under our feet, loud with crickets singing.

Later, I had just showered. My bedroom door locked for the night. A soft knock.

"You? What are you doing in a woman's dorm?" I asked.

He sat on the edge of the bed. "Did you think I was going to let you get away with that?"

"With what? What did I say?" He laughed. Then the struggle between, good and evil must have started in his head. It was in mine. Suddenly, he got up, as if to go. I stood at the door to let him out. But instead of leaving, he changed his mind and kissed me, and we were back down on the bed.

Before I could think of the reasons not to, he kicked off his running shoes.

There are so many memories, scenes that come to mind when I think of him. Walking by the ocean, in the hot sun. The other woman in the class and an older man, a Canadian, with us. I still have the photo of me in my bathing suit, sitting on a yellow beach towel. Somehow, we got away from them and walked along the shore. The tide was out and the water calm. We passed the sign about the dangerous undertow. The tap, where sunbathers washed the sticky salt from their skin. The noisy concession stand that smelled of hot dogs and candy floss. I can still feel the sand between my toes.

"I want to hold your hand," he said. "But I'm afraid someone I know will see us."

That night, I lay naked on my bed and relished the cool air on my red skin. The soft knock. I got up and opened the door.

"My God, is this for me? My wife would never greet me like this."

We whispered, afraid the woman next door might hear. Then he bent over me. His hand trailing along my leg, my inner thigh, and there.

"Now, don't make a sound. Not a single sound."

Afterward, I remembered the story of the Good Samaritan. He finds someone robbed and beaten, half dead on the road. The Samaritan saves him, washes away the blood and pours oil into his wounds.

My lover's semen was my oil.

My memory is fuzzy about the details. We never discussed morality, whether or not it was right or wrong. The Zoroastrians say, "The evil one is best fought by joy. Despondency is a symbol of his victory." I was not sad once, all that hot July and August, even though I knew, when the summer was over, he wouldn't write. "I can't risk a scandal," he said. He had a big congregation in Chicago.

On the last evening, the eleven of us ate at a piano bar. We sat under a stained glass window, a figure of swords crossed. Heavy pine beams above us. The place smelled of wooden wine caskets. We ordered beer. Hot barbecued chicken wings. Or was it potato skins? I chatted with the musician and told him how I had a degree in voice and he invited me to sing. So, I did. *Kiss The Day Goodbye.* My farewell present to Almus. I kept the mike close to my lips and my voice carried straight to our table. I didn't look away from him. My eyes dry, just like the lyrics said.

I came to that phrase, "We did what we had to do and I can't regret what I did for love," and he was smiling at me. Did evil win out between us? His church would have said so.

Afterward, we sat down on that same park bench. Counted the stars, kissed. Then he started fishing in his pockets. "I've got something for you," he said and handed me a small blue box. I lifted the lid. A silver seashell on a chain. Before I could say thank you, his eyes filled with tears. Nobody ever wept at leaving me before—not even my own husband. I don't think anyone has cried over me since.

Wild Life In The Canadian Wilderness

Despite the claims of those who would destroy them coyotes are not vicious animals. As a matter of fact, it is said that they have a sense of humor and have been observed in playful antics.

When I am lonely I walk in the ravine. The knowledge that the trees still stand along the path and over the next rise of hills, still stand regardless of drought, fire and disease, is a symbol of permanence in my own inconstant world. The sun, flickering through leaves and warm on my skin, comforts me.

Sometimes I linger on the balcony of my friend's apartment building and gaze beyond the roof tops to the fringe of trees where the ravine begins. From this perspective I can observe the activity in the woods. A red winged blackbird sits on a reed by the stream and trills a melancholy song. Squirrels jump perilously from one branch to another.

The coyote is linked to black magic and sorcery. For instance, it is said they can hypnotize other animals by waving their tails. They have been known to reward individuals who have saved them from traps or haunt those who have caused them harm.

I am staying in Sister Martha's apartment while she is on retreat. A beige chesterfield with large brown and wine flowers sits on a bright green rug and beside that unmatching turquoise chairs. The windows are hung with striped orange curtains. Outside the sliding door is a bare hot balcony, no cross ventilation. My friend has only gone away for a few weeks but her closets and drawers are empty. One sturdy pair of brown oxfords rests on the closet floor, heels together, toes pointing out, standing in the same position in which she left them.

Above the kitchen table and in the front alcove is a crucifix. The tiny cot in her bedroom, much too small for a man to share, is guarded by a statue of the Virgin standing head bowed, hands clasped. I study Martha's little library: *Women In The Church; The Unremembered Servants; The Gift of Chastity; Brides of Christ.* Pictures of her favorite saints are lined along the hallway in a neat row: Maria Goretti, raped and murdered by a young man, forgave and converted him in a dream while he was still in prison; Saint Adelaide, shut up in a castle because she refused to marry the son of her husband's murderer; Mary of Magdela, remembered in legend as a prostitute because she loved Jesus sensuously. Each of the three canonized for their devotion to a man.

Considered to be the most musical of mammals coyotes have a range of several octaves. Often they howl when they are lonely in order to locate their missing mates.

All around me I hear noises of people and families. A mother shouts at her child to come for dinner. Two voices argue above the music of the stereo. Martha asked me to empty her mail box but the key sticks in the lock and I can't get at her messages even though I bang on the metal door. Soon the box will be full. Then, what will she think of me for not taking care of things?

My mail must be collecting at Pete's place, too. But I won't go back to face him, walk into the room where the sheer curtains flutter in the breeze, steak fries on the barbecue, the radio plays easy listening music and he looks up and smiles, thinking I've relented and come back.

I did not want to go. I wanted to try again, harder.

Most coyotes mate for life and express affection by singing to one another, pawing and nuzzling.

When I unpacked I put a slender bottle of sleeping pills beside Martha's statue of the Madonna in the middle of her bedside table. A doctor gave me the small vial of sedatives after dental surgery a few months ago. I have been saving them. I knew this time would come. I am sinking into my own dark night of the soul. Let me slip into oblivion and find God, but not through prayer and meditation and acceptance of suffering as did the great mystics. My own brand of denial and asceticism offers no ecstasy.

After the ten o'clock news CBC broadcasts a program of jazz. The D.J. has chosen a song from Holly Cole's album, *Girl Talk.* Her husky voice drifts into my reverie, "I'm so lonely I could die."

The night before I left Pete I noticed crumbs on the kitchen floor, a little row of them just under the fridge. I should have taken the broom from the closet and cleaned up before I went to bed.

Although carnivorous, coyotes eat a large amount of vegetation. In some seasons their menu may consist entirely of grass and berries.

Before she went on retreat Martha and I had lunch at her favorite restaurant, an elegant place where we sat and talked surrounded by pretty pink table cloths, crystal and waiters in uniform. I ordered salad and was surprised to find flowers tucked in between the green peppers and lettuce. I nibbled the little orange buds that tasted quite like their color but I could not bring myself to chew the delicate petals. Apparently nasturtiums are a gourmet's delight. I told her about the break-up, that all my clothes were piled into the trunk of my car and I had nowhere to go. That was when she offered to let me stay in her apartment.

She says that an organized exterior often means a disorganized interior. "It sounds like he was obsessive-compulsive." She talks softly, making tentative suggestions, not pronouncements. But she knows. She's a psychologist with a Ph.D. "If you had stayed any longer the fights might have escalated," she says. "He might have become physical."

But now it's I who want to attack him. I want to howl, rage, scratch and tear at the limbs I once loved to caress.

The coyote is a carnivorous predator who stalks his prey with patience and cunning.

After the first week of unpacking and settling, I stayed in the apartment as little as possible. I went back to the ravine where Pete and I used to wander. We took picnics there, made love under a tree.

Once when we were driving past the ravine where it rambles beyond the outskirts of the city, we saw an elk being chased by a pack of coyotes. He was on the edge of the woods, just behind a row of cedars, and Pete slowed down so we were going at the same pace as the animal that was being chased. One coyote snapped at his heels while the other stayed a few paces behind. Then another would catch up and relieve his mate. The elk, running for his life, moved gracefully. At one point he turned and tried to kick the coyote but missed. Then he bolted into the thicket, the pack chasing after.

"Do you think he'll get away?" I asked.

"No," said Pete. "They singled him out for a reason. Must be old and tired."

Lately, I am spending more and more time in the ravine. I sit and think about Pete, about how he isn't as handsome as when I first met him, that his hair is receding and his belly developing a pot. I read my book, *Wild Life In The Canadian Wilderness,* for hours under a tree. All afternoon until the sun sets I lounge on the cool dank earth cushioned by weeds and flowers and I taste berries, their purple juices staining my lips and dribbling down my chin.

When I first went to Martha's I tried to forgive Pete for all the pain he had caused, to pray magnanimously as did Saint Maria Goretti. I hid myself in Martha's apartment away from the whole world in the style of Saint Adelaide. I tried to be like Mary of Magdela and forget Pete's touch. But I am not saint material.

Sometimes when I go to the ravine I don't think about Pete at all but about coyotes. I study the photographs, their long sleek muscular bodies, intelligent faces, narrow sharp eyes. I shake my head as they do when insects bother me. I grin up at them but my lips have narrowed and tightened so that my teeth are bared. Frightened, they scatter.

The coyote has large strong jaws and teeth like shears that are capable of cutting away large chunks of flesh, which may be gulped down without chewing.

Now, I only go back to the apartment in the daytime. I prefer to sleep in the forest at night. During one of these moonlight reveries, I plan my revenge.

It's not hard to lure Pete into the ravine. I phone him at work and even though my voice is hoarse and rasping he recognizes it and says, "I was waiting for your call." He thinks it's another reconciliation like all the other ones we've had before. He even brings a blanket to spread under the tree. "God, I've missed you," he says.

When he arrives, he stands under the tree, checks his watch, shakes his head and I can hear him thinking, "She's late again." The wool covering hanging over his arms reeks of detergent but as he unfolds it and settles down yawning and stretching to wait for me, I can smell the fragrant scent of sheep, or is it the odour of his flesh, dank and animal?

When at last I approach, moving out from the shadows of leaves and branches he gasps, starts. I duck behind a tree. Have I changed that much?

"Who's there?" he says. He backs away calling, "Hello?" There is a tremor in his voice and he staggers and nearly falls, his feet twisted in the blanket. I can feel my heart pounding as it used to when his hand slid down my leg. My face is hot in the cool wash of moonlight, my throat dry. I want to call out his name but my lips will not cooperate. A dog barks and I can only hear its yapping in my ears. I come out from my hiding place and imagine sliding up against him, curling around his body. He smells so sweetly.

"My God! Is it you?" He takes one look at me and starts to run. Doesn't he recognize me? I head him off from the path that leads to the highway and he rushes pell-mell into the bushes. Unused to the terrain he stumbles and falls. I let him recover, even get a head start and then I'm after him again. He looks over his shoulder and I see the terror in his eyes and I want to laugh because that's the way I used to look at him when he would get into one of his rages. All through the night I run him down, over rocks, fallen trees, dry creek beds. Branches scratch at his eyes, gnarled roots catch his feet. He falls more than once and the last time stays down. I circle around him, my feet padding softly in the grass. Then his eyes open and he screams, raises his arms to fend me off and bolts down the hill towards the river and the thickest part of the forest. I try to call his name, to wrap my tongue around the vowels and consonants but only a melancholy howl follows him into the darkness.

In the early morning I arrive back at the apartment. Exhausted but content, I sprawl on the rug to sleep under the watchful eyes of the saints. But they no longer outstare me from their picture frames.

I may not be canonized but I am revenged.

II
Through the Jungle

The night was just ending
and the city had already begun to stir,
the brightening streets already raucous
with jeepneys and people rushing to
escape the traffic mess that surely
would come with daylight.

He strained to remember
the fallow fields, the little towns,
but the pictures that came to
mind were indistinct.

F. Sionil José

Promise

The ravine, beside my little cottage, sloped into a verdant jungle thick with creeping vines and branches. I burned the garbage on a spot as far away from the house as possible. Still, the smell drifted in between the open slats. Each time I struck a match to light the waste, I remembered the fragrance of burning autumn leaves back home in Alberta and the smell of smoke flying out of the chimney, from the wood stove, on a crisp winter night. But this stench was overpowering.

Professor Jenkins had warned me about culture shock. He cleared his throat as he did when he was about to give a lecture. "No matter how well traveled you think you are, expect to go through a period of depression when you arrive in the Philippines," he had said.

"I can handle it."

I knew about loneliness. Nothing could be worse than the sick feeling that had engulfed me as I watched my son climb into his truck and head out for Vancouver. I was divorced when Matt was only five years old, and I had raised him. Just finished high school, he was on his way to study percussion at Capilano College.

Having survived the deafening roar of rock in our basement when he was young, I thanked God when he suddenly acquired a love for Jazz. Then, on my birthday, he gave me a set of tapes I could play in my car while I drove back and forth to work.

"I think you'll like this," he grinned as I opened up the present.

"Beethoven Sonatas. Wonderful. What a gift."

"Maybe you'd rather have had Chopin," he said with a newly acquired, sophisticated air.

What do you do when your only son leaves home? Fling your arms about him and cry, realizing those precious and frightening years are flying away in the spray of gravel and exhaust fumes? Or be brave and promise yourself a new life, as the feminists say in all the books on menopause.

I refused to be a possessive mother or a tearful woman going through mid-life crises, so I grabbed at the chance to take a sabbatical away from the college where I taught psychology. A small Protestant university outside of Manila invited me to teach basic counselling skills to young men and women preparing for the ministry. I had no worries about fitting into the seminary even though I'm not particularly churchgoing. I had been married in the United Church of Canada and Matt was baptized there. I took him to Sunday School when he was little, but after the divorce, I felt uncomfortable surrounded by all the good married couples. We drifted away, but I kept my faith.

Communication wasn't going to be a problem, either. Although the national language of the Philippines is Tagalog, all the students could write and speak English. A good education was the result of the Americans' occupation after the war.

"Ma'am, you're the best American teacher we've ever had," said Jestril, one of the students.

"Thanks," I said.

"Yeah. We understand you. You pronounce your words clearly."

"Actually, I'm Canadian."

"I didn't know there was a difference."

"Oh, yes. We're a separate country. But we're a bit like the Filipinos. We're always trying to find our identity. You see, our roots are British and French…."

"It must be your English accent then."

"Oh, I've never been to England."

When I first met Jestril, he was playing in a student concert. I listened to the music as I had at Matt's recitals: a faltering version of Chopin's *Minute Waltz*, a soprano's shrill attempt at Gounod's *Ave Maria* and a robust version of *Amazing Grace* sung by the choir.

The concert took place in the Salakot Chapel, a circular building with a dome roof designed to look like the hat peasants wear in the rice paddies. Since there were no walls, dogs were free to wander in and out and birds flew up to the rafters in the ceiling. One of the students, an artist, had painted a mural at the front of the sanctuary, a pastoral scene of farmers working in the fields. The workers were shaded, not by a green tree, but by a bare brown cross that reached up into the sky. The rest of the building, in poor repair, badly needed a paint job.

When Jestril came forward, the students burst into applause. He lifted his trombone to his lips, and a sweet mournful melody filled the air. He was taller than the average Filipino and made an imposing figure. He closed his eyes, bent low and then, with a graceful sweep, lifted his head high, blowing the notes into the heavens. His throat and the shiny brass musical instrument became one, like a swan singing its last song.

The students gave him a standing ovation, and to my great embarrassment I wanted to cry. After that, he played *Summertime* and *Some Enchanted Evening*, old and beautiful American show tunes. But neither was as sensuous as that Filipino love song.

The next day I had planned an exercise for the class.

"Today, I want you to draw your family tree as far back as you can go. Who were the heroes and who were the villains among your ancestors?" My reasoning was to help them begin to understand some of their family myths and symbols, so that they could appreciate the effect of this on their own lives and, some day, on the lives of their parishioners.

They giggled and apologized, for this one's uncle had been killed because of a gambling debt. "Yes, he was a villain," smirked one of the students, enjoying his roguish background. Someone else's grandmother came from one of the indigenous tribes in the north. She held the family together when the parents went to work in Japan. "Most certainly she was the hero," the class agreed. When Jestril came forward, he hesitated and spoke in a near whisper, so that I could scarcely hear. Gone was the authority and presence of the night before.

"My father died in a typhoon when I was just a boy. So my mother left the provinces and went to Manila to live with her father. She was a fish vendor. My granddaddy played in a swing band. He taught me all about the music business before he died. Then, my mother lost the fish business. So, I played in bars to get money to eat. But she didn't like that. I didn't drink. But my granddaddy did. My mother got sick and on her death bed made me promise I wouldn't follow him but go into the church, instead. Now, I'm trying to help my people."

"So, in your own family, who might you say is the villain?"

Jestril shrugged. "My granddaddy. He drank."

"True. But he did teach you to play." I imagined the old fellow in the empty bar, before the rehearsals on a Saturday morning. His little grandson, legs swinging, sits on the high piano bench and picks out a song with one finger for his grandfather.

"My mother. She worked hard. Raised us. She'd be the hero in the family," Jestril continued.

"If drinking wasn't a problem for you, wouldn't you make more money as a musician? I mean, instead of going into the church."

"I promised," he said.

I traveled to Mindoro during the student's reading week, and stayed in a beautiful resort built high up in the mountains. The tourists were housed in little huts on bamboo stilts, overlooking the ocean. Palm trees towered and swayed above us. Their heavy, broad leaves were used to decorate our dinner plates at night. The dining room, surrounded by torches, was located down the mountain by the pool. The path that led to it, though treacherous, was lit with flares and bounded by a rope hand rail. I arrived just in time for dinner.

The waiter seated me near a young Australian couple, on their honeymoon. "I'll have what they're eating," I said. "Looks delicious."

"*Morcon*, it's the cook's specialty. Marinated beef, rolled up like a jelly roll and stuffed with bell peppers and sweet pickles," said the waiter.

"Sounds good."

"We serve it only on festive occasions."

"Well, I'm on a holiday now," I said.

After I had gone back up to the hillside to bed, the rain started. Howling wind woke me up in the middle of the night. My little hut swayed like the tall palm trees. There was no door, only two flaps made of some flimsy material that had been lightly hooked together. Now they flew like rags in a gale. I caught the ends, stuck them together with a safety pin, and went back to bed with a pillow over my head.

I dreamed my hut had been torn from its poles and my bed, like a sleigh with me still on my stomach, slithered down the mountain in a mudslide. I woke up before we crashed to the bottom and lay in bed, afraid to venture down the mountain to the sturdy main building. I looked outside and saw the trees uprooted and the rope handrail dragging in the mud. I thought about Jestril and his family in their frail shelter. The next day newspapers were full of stories about people who had been killed in the typhoon.

It was in such a storm that Jestril's father had died.

A few weeks later, in the town of Dasmarinas, not the rich suburb of Manila that bears the same name, but the village near the university, I bought *bangus*, a kind of fish and crabs from a vendor. She sat beside her wares, under an awning and brushed flies away with a listless motion, apparently unaware of the stench. Her bright yellow dress hung on her bones and dragged in the dirt. I couldn't bear to haggle with her but paid what she demanded. She smiled broadly, unabashed that her two front teeth were missing. "*Paalam*, thank you," I said, as I walked away with my purchase.

Is that how Jestril's mother looked, eking out a living for her son?

One day Jestril came to me after class. He wore the same old faded green T-shirt that must have been washed every night before he went to bed.

"Ma'am, could I be excused for a week?. There's a gig in Manila. I need the money and...."

"Of course. I'll tell you what to read so you don't get behind."

"Thanks, Ma'am. I thought about what you said. About the music and not letting it go."

He came back to school in the middle of the week.

"Back so soon? How was the gig?" I said.

"Finished."

"But I thought it was for a whole week."

"I had to give the trombone back. My friend needed it."

"But where's yours?"

"I don't own one. I sold it to come to school."

I spent part of the Christmas holidays in Manila. Roxas Boulevard, the wide main thoroughfare that looks out onto the bay, is pretty, but the narrow side streets smell of urine and garbage. Since friends had warned me to dress poorly because of pickpockets, I took off my gold earrings and wore blue jeans. Nervous at being a woman alone, I dodged in and out of stores so that I would be around people. I wasn't really looking for a trombone, but the city was full of second hand shops, many of them with guitars hanging in the windows. When I saw the instrument gleaming on a dusty shelf, I had to buy it. I could see Jestril playing on a cruise ship somewhere, or in one of those fancy American hotels. He would never be hungry again.

He opened the gift after class when the other students had gone. "Ma'am, that's too much."

"Now you can be a real musician," I said. "Why don't you go to Manila after Christmas? Look up some of your grandfather's old friends."

He stroked the trombone lying across his knee.

Before I left the Philippines, I drew the course to a close by asking the students to create a poem, a drawing, or a song that expressed some new concept that they had learned.

"We'll sing you something, Ma'am," said one of the girls.

"No, each one of you must create something that tells me about your own understanding. It's worth ten marks."

"No. We'll do it together. Put it on tape. Our gift to you," said another. The class nodded in agreement.

I relented.

On the last day of classes, I held a *merienda*, a party, in my little cottage. Two old and broken arm chairs and three wicker chairs stood around the only table. So, the students sat on the hard floor on a woven mat made of dried grass, or remained standing and leaned against the walls. Wanting to offer them something nourishing and different, I cooked rice pudding full of sweetened condensed milk and raisins. I had no idea of its culinary history, but I pretended this was Canadian fare. Though they ate rice at nearly every meal, they had never tasted this dish.

Towards the end of the afternoon, one of the young men said, "Ma'am, we'd like to wish you good-bye." They joined hands and made a circle around me and prayed in Tagalog and English. I don't remember all the words now, but I know they prayed for a safe journey and my well being. Then they presented me with the creative project I had asked for, a tape they had made of their singing.

"Oh, thanks. I'll enjoy playing this in my car when I drive to work. Now tell me. Where are your churches? Where will you go when you graduate?"

One by one they answered, "Back to the provinces." "Manila." "Baguio."

The months had flown by since Christmas, and I wondered if Jestril had taken my suggestion and found work with his new trombone. "What will you do when school is finished?" I asked him.

"I'll be ordained right away."

"Really?" I covered my disappointment with another question. "What church are they sending you to? Do you know?"

"Smoky Mountain," he said.

"I see." I stopped eating and put the unfinished bowl of rice pudding on the table.

"I promised, Ma'am."

I wished him happiness. What else could I do?

"We'll sing for you now," said one of the students.

"The song we recorded. Your gift," said another.

Jestril picked up his trombone. Smoky Mountain is a garbage dump outside Manila where poor people scavenge through heaps of refuse and children, bare-foot, play on broken glass, their eyes stinging, their throats dry with the stench of burning garbage. The government doesn't allow tourists to go there. I read somewhere that the image of Hell was based on nothing more than the garbage dump outside Jerusalem.

Then I recognized the plaintive strains of the beautiful Filipino love song that had moved me on the night of the concert. Jestril lifted the trombone to his lips and blew into its golden throat. The instrument seemed to come alive in his hands. He played in harmony with the singing, and swayed to the rhythm like a primitive shaman in a trance. Floating into the evening air, the melody wafted above the palm trees, drifted past the skyscrapers and American hotels, mingled with the salty ocean breeze and city smoke. The cicadas' hum and dogs' bark, the flies' buzz and fish vendors' sing-song cry, all drowned in his mournfully sweet wail of song.

Two Sisters

Miranda gained weight with each pregnancy. The two girls, Blessing and Alleluia, came within about nine months of each other and then, a few anxious years later, her son, José. Pedro said he loved every pound, every inch of his wife. He drove a truck for a beer company and made deliveries up and down the coast from Belair to Manila. Since the trip took a couple of weeks, it was always a real fiesta when he came home. Miranda never worried about him. He knew every curve and boulder on the mountain roads. When he stopped in Belair, his cousin, who owned a small hotel, made sure that he was well fed. He would rest a day or two, play *madyong* with the men in the afternoon and get rid of the last load before nightfall.

The floods during the rainy season caused the accident. According to witnesses, Pedro had eased the truck through a stream but this time, while swerving out of the muck back on to the gravel road, the vehicle tilted sideways, and turned over. The empty beer crates tumbled over the rocks, down into the ravine, and the truck slid after them.

He stayed in the hospital for a month. The medical bills and drugs he had to take (and still takes for the pain) took everything the family owned and more. Pedro's cousin in Belair helped with some of the expenses and the members of the church bought his wheelchair. Still they went into debt and the two girls had to leave school.

Desperate, Miranda tried everything to make her husband well again. She even took him to Christosomo, a faith healer. Some of the people in the village believed that the Virgin gave him the gift of healing when he was a young man. For a long time he traveled about and then settled in Maria, where even the most cynical had to admit that more than one person benefited from his piety.

They waited patiently in the chapel for Christosomo to return from lunch. Miranda stared at a statue of the virgin in her long gold dress. On the walls were framed pictures of the healer, his arms around smiling and grateful people he had helped. There were even photos of his own crucifixion, a ritual he endured with other holy men who gathered in the province at Easter. Half empty bottles contained oils which he used in certain healing ceremonies, and used candles leaned against a shelf dripping with wax. After Christosomo had examined Pedro, he didn't ask for any money, tell him to light a candle or sacrifice a chicken. He ran his hand over the invalid's face and touched his knees and lifeless legs and shook his head. "A little gin every morning will chase the pain away," was all he said.

Eventually, Miranda and her children got used to Pedro just sitting in a stupor in his wheelchair and staring through the window at nothing. His mother came to live with them and help out. She fed her son and cleaned up after him, so that Miranda could work. She took in laundry, but she couldn't make enough to feed six mouths.

Just about that time the recruiter came to the village and spoke to some of the high school students about the big restaurant in Seoul. José tore home, dust flying under his running shoes. "Jobs, Ma. I could be a bus boy." One of his cousins worked in a restaurant in Manila at a five star hotel. He had seen photographs of the young man in his white uniform balancing a tray of empty glasses over his head.

Miranda scarcely had a chance to tidy up before the recruiter arrived at the house. She pushed the laundry basket behind the door. But he wasn't interested in José. "Too young," he said, a gold tooth flashing as he smiled. He spoke better English than most Filipinos and painted quite a picture about the life of waitresses connected with the restaurant in Korea. He talked about the days off, the chances to explore the city, and the generous patrons who came from all over the world: Taiwan, Australia, Hong Kong and the United States.

"Good tips," he said, winking at the girls. He held the coffee cup between finely tapered fingers, clean nails and rings. His gold watch and wrist band flashed when he raised the cup to his mouth. "Delicious coffee."

Miranda wiped away the beads of perspiration that had formed on her upper lip. "More?" she said holding up the half empty pot.

She had read newspaper reports about a girl who had gone to work in Manila. Was she a waitress? A chamber maid? She died of an infection.

"No thanks. I must be going." The smoke from his cigarette escaped between his lips and out his nose as he spoke.

There was something stuck in the girl's vagina. They didn't charge the man with rape because she had just had her thirteenth birthday and was of the age of consent.

"Please. Think about my offer," said the recruiter.

The girl was too embarrassed to tell anyone, until the pain got so bad.

He got up to leave. Alleluia rose politely from her chair but looked away from him, over her shoulder to where Pedro was sitting and nodding. Blessing giggled and shook his hand when he got up to leave.

"So far away," said Miranda.

"They could come home at Christmas," he smiled.

Miranda counted the months as she moved toward the door. But he had already opened it and was letting himself out.

"*Magandang gabi*," he said. "Good evening."

"They're good children," said Pedro's mother as she cleaned up the coffee cups. "They won't do anything wrong."

The next week José and Miranda took the girls to the bus depot. The recruiter paid for their tickets right from Maria to Seoul. Miranda wanted to swallow them with her eyes. As long as they were in her sight, they would be safe. Alleluia's black hair was caught in a bow at the nape of her neck. As she squeezed past the soft drinks vendor and the evangelist shouting out Bible verses into a microphone, the ribbon fell from her hair. Alleluia reached back and grabbed for it but it was too late. The red bow was caught and torn under the wheels of a passing jeepney. Blessing waved good-bye at the top of the stairs and Alleluia smoothed her unruly hair back, behind her ears. José threw kisses. Miranda felt sick to her stomach. "It must be the *bangus*," she said. "With the bus lurching as it does the girls will surely be ill."

Their last supper together consisted of a few pieces of fish and some rice wrapped in banana leaves. Miranda put the leftovers in a paper bag so the girls would have something to eat on their long trip. She held a kerchief to her mouth as the bus rolled away in a cloud of exhaust fumes. José ran down the road until they were out of sight. She ran to the public toilet. It was locked. So she threw up behind an acacia tree.

The checks come monthly. Postcards of Seoul. Friends begin talking about the possibility of Pedro going to the States for an operation. The girls are making that much money. "See, no need to worry," says Pedro's mother.

On Christmas Eve, Miranda goes to the airport. She wears a jacket for the bus ride from Maria—eight hours and then the jeepney ride to the outskirts of Manila. But she finds the city heat oppressive as she is used to mountain air.

Blessing and Alleluia will never be able to find me in the crowd, she thinks. She wishes she had enough *pesos* to bribe one of the guards so that she could get past the barrier that separates the passengers from their relatives and friends.

Feeling lightheaded, she holds a handkerchief to her mouth. The fat man behind Miranda rubs against her ample buttocks as he strains to see over her shoulder into the crowd. Maybe the girls' holidays were cancelled. Busy restaurant. Lots of tips, she thinks. She reads the wrist watch on the fat man's hand. Maybe they missed their plane. A thin woman's elbow jabs the fatty part of her arm. Miranda tries to move away but there is a young man beside her, holding up a sign with someone's name painted in red. She puts her hand to her throat to quell the growing nausea. Where are they? She scans the crowd.

She presses up against the barrier, clutching the wire, her fingers marked red as she shakes the fence at oncoming passengers.

Head Hunters

At first, Beatrice refused to go to the Philippines with her new husband Jim McCauley. But he had promised himself in his youth, that after the war, he would go back to Manila. "I want to see the country in peace time," he said. The years had crawled by and now, at the age of seventy with a woman twenty years his junior, he decided to fulfill that vow.

"It's not the sort of place you go on a holiday." complained Beatrice. She remembered all those terrible stories about Marcos, the torture and imprisonment of innocent people.

"For heaven's sake. The country's stable now," Jim said. "Marcos is dead."

"But there might be some sort of uprising," she answered. She wanted to stay in Canada, where everything was familiar and where she felt safe. She would have preferred to explore the old part of Quebec City or eat lobster near Peggy's Cove.

What had finally clinched the trip, convinced Beatrice she would enjoy the Philippines, was that Jim promised to take her to a psychic healer. She had read about them in a book by Shirley MacLaine.

"I'd like to see one of their surgeries. I want to watch, with my own eyes, their hands go through somebody's flesh and take out the poison."

"Maybe, he could do something for my arthritis," said Jim.

"Yes, or help me sleep," she said.

Beatrice couldn't shake off her anxiety about being in a foreign country so far away from home. They landed in the airport in Manila at night. Crowds of people, who had come to meet family or friends, were lined up against a rope that barricaded them from the arrivals section. They shouted, waved their hand and held up posters.

"I'm glad I don't have to meet anyone, here," she said to Jim. "How do they find each other?" They searched among a pile of suitcases for their baggage.

She began to feel faint with the heat and the air redolent of human sweat, urine, exotic flowers, garbage and gas fumes from the taxis just outside.

"I thought you were a sophisticated traveller," he teased.

The next morning they boarded a small ferry which took them to the island of Corregidor where the Americans and Filipinos had held out against the Japanese troops. The tiny boat rocked on the ocean and the waves flooded over the window obscuring the glimpse of their destination.

"Wait until you see the tunnels where they kept supplies and ammunitions. There's even a hospital where I worked," said Jim.

But Beatrice's face was white. Her mouth, bright with lipstick, a thin red line. The wrinkles on her forehead, creamed away each evening, even more pronounced. "Don't be scared," said Jim as he put his arm around her.

The tunnels were a disappointment. Jim stood in his stripped shorts, his bare legs thin as a bird's and his arms, once muscled, dangling at his side. The maze of passageways, where fallen soldiers had been carried and where Red Cross nurses had bandaged their wounds and looked at the creased photos the boys carried of their mothers and girlfriends back home, had been closed off. Two white boards, nailed together in a large X, like a great bandage, sealed off the dark cavity which led to the various tunnels. There was only one opening where Jim could stand and imagine the sights and sounds of war.

Beatrice shivered and pulled her sweater around her shoulders. The air was cool in comparison to the heat outside but the atmosphere was dank and the gray rock walls confining. "It must have been awful," she said.

"Yes, it was." Jim hadn't seen the worst of the action. He was shipped out before the bloody struggle began. But he had assisted one of the medics, carried an amputated leg off the makeshift operating table, emptied bedpans and cleaned up vomit and blood.

Beatrice stood beside him in respectful silence for a few moments and then took his arm. "Why don't we go back to the hotel? So much more pleasant, there."

Later, they sat by the pool, drank beer, watched birds fly by and gazed at flowers whose names he had forgotten.

"How charming. I had no idea it would be like this. I half expect Cary Grant to walk down the stairs in full uniform," she said. "Don't you?" The interior of the hotel was of dark polished mahogany and there was a grand circular staircase that dominated the lobby.

"It's got a thirties feel to it." He set his drink down, reached over and squeezed her shoulder. "Like a movie set." He kept the conversation going about the hotel's decor. Any inane chatter was better than talk about the war. "Tomorrow, it's your turn," he said.

The day after they had stood at the entrance of the closed-off tunnels, they left Corregidor, caught an air conditioned bus back to Manila and then took a jeepney up to Baguio in the northern part of the province. They sat thigh to thigh with women in colourful skirts and men in short-sleeved shirts, damp with sweat. They were packed solid on benches that lined the two sides of the interior, with parcels and suitcases at their feet. A rooster, a cock fighter, stood poised on the lap of an elderly man with a wrinkled face and a nose that looked like a beak. He fixed his gaze on Beatrice as if ready to pounce. She edged even closer to her husband.

Newspapers were full of stories about bandits with brown paper bags over their faces. They stopped the jeepneys in the mountains and robbed the passengers, even their own countrymen, of wallets and watches. Beatrice heard even worse reports about how foreigners were being scammed. Filipinos, dressed in business suits, stopped visitors and demanded to see their passports. Posing as immigration officials, they threatened to take the unsuspecting tourists to the police station if they didn't immediately pay a fine for not having certain official papers, which didn't exist, on their person.

"We should have phoned somebody back home. Told them our itinerary," she said as they bumped and jerked their way up a narrow road.

"We don't have an itinerary."

"We should have one."

"Why?" asked Jim.

"In case something happens to us."

Jim shrugged and took her hand. "We're okay."

The jeepney, lights flashing, horn blasting, sped by peasants plodding behind their *carabeos*, slowly overturning the wet black earth. A troop of school girls dressed in gray uniforms got on board. They had to stand or perch themselves on the boxes and crates. One of them nearly fell into Beatrice's lap as the jeepney lurched forward. "Sorry. Did I step on your toes?"

"Not at all." The girl's hand was light on Beatrice's arm as she tried to steady herself.

"Where are you going?" asked the girl.

"Baguio."

"The mountains. You'll like it there. Nice and cool."

Beatrice forgot about the stories of bandits as the girl and her friends chattered about the delights of Baguio.

"You must go to the weaver's shop. Get yourself a jacket for the night air. And the silversmith."

At noon they came to a bus station and everyone sought out the washrooms or restaurants. Beatrice followed several of the women to a small hut. A crone in a faded flowered sundress, which revealed her boney shoulders, held the door open and ushered Beatrice in, while the rest stood back. It took a minute for her eyes to become accustomed to the darkness. First, Beatrice noticed a trough at the base of the floor that ran around the room. Must be for drainage, she thought and looked up at the ceiling to see where rainwater might leak through holes. Then she saw the toilet, a large, white and cracked bowl with neither seat nor lid. Carefully, she put her purse on the floor, pulled down her underthings and perched herself on the edge. Suddenly she realized she was not alone. The women had come in behind her and were squatting over the trough urinating. The old one in the sundress picked up her purse and thrust it into Beatrice's lap. "Dirty, dirty," she said pointing to the floor. Beatrice could do nothing but smile and nod her thank you's as she relieved herself sitting on the toilet high above the group of women. They smiled back.

Jim met her at the parked jeepney and handed her a coke.

"You'll never guess what happened," she said and told him about the shared washroom facilities.

"Good. Now you're all acquainted."

As they continued their journey, the jeepney became even more crowded. Boys, sitting on top of the luggage strapped to the roof, dangled their legs in the windows. When Beatrice and Jim arrived in Baguio and alighted from the bus, they were met by a group of men who wore headdresses of white feathers. "Wood carving?" said one of them brandishing his workmanship at Beatrice.

"What have you got there?" she asked.

He held up a souvenir, an ugly face with exaggerated ears and mouth turned downward. "Spirits, demons," answered the man.

"These people are Igorots," said the jeepney driver. "Belong to the mountain tribes. Used to be head hunters. They believed the spirit of a dead comrade would haunt his relatives until his enemies had been killed and decapitated."

The next day they went to see the psychic surgeon. He lived in a modern apartment complex high on a hill which overlooked the city. An ordinary looking man, he wore a plaid cotton shirt and a baseball cap which he took off as he waved to the couple. "Enteng's my name," he said as they shook hands. "Can I get you a coke, beer?"

"No, thanks," said Jim. "We're from Calgary and my wife has done a bit of reading about psychic surgeons."

"We're interested in your work," said Beatrice.

"You have a good baseball team, there."

"Good enough, I suppose," said Jim.

"My husband suffers from arthritis," said Beatrice.

"I collect baseball pins. See." He took of his hat and showed them an array of ornaments he had stuck around the brim.

"We were wondering if you're doing any surgeries at this time," said Beatrice.

"No, I've just come back from a holiday in England."

"I see," said Jim. "What part?"

"London, my nephew has a restaurant."

"So, I suppose there's nothing you could do for my arthritis."

"Keep your jacket on. It gets cold here at night. Mountain air."

"Well, I guess we should be moving along." Jim got up from his chair.

"Sorry. This isn't my busiest time of year." They started walking towards the door. "I did a curse for a man the other day. That's about all."

"You did a curse?" said Beatrice. She stopped on the top step and wheeled about. "You actually put curses on people?"

"You have a wonderful view," said Jim as the two men shook hands.

Beatrice couldn't sleep that night. Once in New Orleans she had visited the Voodoo Museum. She was fascinated by the fact that pins stuck in a doll, in just the right spots, could cause the death of an enemy.

Her friend, a nurse, had told her about a patient from Africa. "Before he came to Canada he had slept with his best friend's wife. The woman's husband found out and put a hex on him. The doctors in the intensive care couldn't do a thing for the poor man. Imagine a curse having that much power all the way across the ocean."

"I want to curse Ray," said Beatrice. She was sitting up on the edge of the bed, hunched over, staring at the chipped red nail polish on her toes. "Do you think I'm crazy?"

When Jim first met Beatrice, she was given to fits of crying. Friday nights, after work, she drove to Nanton, a small town outside of Calgary where he lived. He cooked her gourmet dinners, a leg of lamb or B.C. salmon, made a pitcher of martinis. In the morning, he brought her breakfast on a silver tray. She ate toast and honey and sipped coffee, while reading a spy story *China Lake*, a gift she had given him after their first weekend together.

"This is like a holiday," she said.

Each Friday night he changed the bed and exchanged cotton pillowcases for satin ones. "You need pampering," he said.

Sometimes, when she arrived in his apartment, she was as pale as if she had seen a ghost and her hands were cold and shaky. As soon as she had exited off the Deerfoot Trail, which carried most of the city traffic, her mind became like a T.V. screen filled with unwanted images.

"I can see that bastard sticking his penis in my boy's mouth." Jim helped her take off her coat. "What if he caused Stephen pain?" Sometimes the martinis changed her mood from a holiday one to black depression.

"Don't talk to me about love," she said as he began unbuttoning her blouse. "I worshipped Ray. I never dreamed he'd go after my child." She pushed Jim away and swept the glass pitcher full of melting ice cubes off the coffee table. "May he rot in hell for touching my baby."

Jim met Stephen only once. He was fourteen and like many Canadian boys played hockey but secretly he preferred chess, so Jim found out after Stephen beat him royally.

"Who taught you to play like that?"

"Ray, Mom's old boyfriend."

Then suddenly Stephen went to Vancouver to live with his dad. Jim didn't get a chance to say good-bye.

"Can you believe he was an A student once?" They were having coffee in Jim's kitchen. "He's skipped so many classes he can't get back into some of them," said Beatrice. She hugged herself with her arms. "He'll do better living with his dad and going to a new school."

Jim went over to her and, not knowing what else to do, he patted her back.

"I went to Ray for counselling after the divorce and then he became my lover. I was so lonely."

"He hit on your boy, too?"

"I swear to God, I didn't know."

"Can you take him to court? Did you go to the police?"

"The crown wouldn't take the case. Stephen's word against Ray's. Then when it all came out, when Stephen told me, he became suicidal. I had to put him in the hospital."

Jim put his arm around her and she was leaning into him crying and choking.

"It's all my fault. I should never have got involved with him. Brought him into the house."

"Easy." Jim left her for a moment and went to the washroom for a cold cloth. He watched the water gush from the silver faucet. He used to fill buckets of water when he was in the army, washed bandages full of blood and puss and diapers stinking of excrement. Only those belonged to a fourteen-year-old Filipino boy who had been sodomized so often and so cruelly, he has lost control of his sphincter muscles. His mother had somehow got him to an American doctor in Corregidor.

Jim gathered the wet cloth in his hands, knelt down and wiped her forehead and her red face.

Jim phoned Enteng and explained who Beatrice wanted cursed and why.

"It'll cost a hundred American dollars and you'll need to bring a few things. A plucked chicken, a bottle of red wine and thirteen new *pesos*."

Jim shook his head and hung up the phone. "He'll see us this afternoon. First we have to go to the market."

The ritual of the curse took place in Enteng's kitchen. There was no thunder or lightning and the room was well lit with electricity. Beatrice wrote Ray's full name on a piece of paper and then burnt it in candle flames. Enteng caught the ashes in a saucer and threw them on a piece of white cloth. Then he put the *pesos* in a circle around the ashes. "You're sure you don't have a picture or something that belongs to him?"

"No," said Beatrice.

"Too bad. The curse would be stronger, then." He closed his eyes and muttered something in Tagalog. "The second part I do tonight at the stroke of twelve."

Yeah. The second part is drinking the bottle of wine, thought Jim.

"The chicken must be cooked and offered to the spirits," Entang said.

Later, at the hotel, Beatrice laughed. "How could I have been so stupid! What a waste of money."

"Has it made you feel any better?"

"Yes," she said and then wistfully, "I wish I'd had a photograph."

Bahala Na

When the letter from Rita came, I could have cried. It brought back so many happy memories of my Filipino students. I still think of them, when I sit and sip sherry by my crackling fire in the middle of the cold Alberta winter. We had so many good times. For six months I lived in the country and taught basic psychology to young ministers about to graduate from seminary and go out to serve their first churches. I tried to teach them western expertise, but I learned more than I taught.

Four young people stand out in my mind. Rita, plain looking and with short black hair, was one of the few unmarried girls in the class. Robert, the oldest student, took it upon himself to help me understand the culture. Married to a sickly woman, he was often absent from class in order to take care of his wife. Lorina, sweet and softly spoken, had more insight than the others realized. Finally, there was Remelita, whom I never met, but whose presence dominated our small classroom and the minds and fantasies of all of us, including myself.

One of the requirements of my course was that each student present a case or a problem one of their parishioners had brought to them. The class would then explore ways of helping their clients to make creative decisions. Though they were eager pupils, some of them were shy about presenting their papers in class.

"Please don't worry so much," I told them. "We are all here to learn."

Then, Robert took me aside and said, "They're afraid of losing face, Ma'am. As ministers of God, they must give the right advice to their parishioners."

I thanked him. I wanted to remind him that a good counsellor doesn't preach, but I held my tongue. Rita, an avid student, presented her case, first.

Rita

"Victor Montero worshipped his wife, Remelita. Since his grandmother belonged to one of the northern tribes, he was dark skinned and heavy set. Strong as a *carabao*, good looking too. He was a graduate of the military college and had taken up weight lifting, so you'd never guess he was in his early fifties, twice the age of his wife. One night he caught Remelita flirting with some man in the bar. He hauled the fellow off his stool and somehow in the scuffle the unlucky man fell down and split his head open. Victor, charged with manslaughter, was given a fifteen year sentence. In just a few months, Remelita was involved with young Julius. He wasn't even twenty-one.

"He was the only one of six children who had finished high school. His mother wanted him to go to college and become a pharmacist but his father had a stroke, that summer, and Julius had to take over their small farm. Everyone knew that he was heartbroken when his father died. They had worked side by side in the rice fields. On holidays, they went to soccer games and cheered for the same team until their voices were hoarse. Someone said they even went to a whorehouse together, but I don't believe that. No wonder he turned to Remelita for comfort. She was more like a mother figure to him. But as she was an experienced woman, he was soon in her clutches. She became his addiction and he couldn't break free."

"You'd think she was a witch. I don't know her well, but you do her an injustice," interrupted Robert.

"She is. She's possessed by spirits," said Rita.

Robert had everyone's attention so he took up the thread of the story.

Robert

"I met Remelita in the store where she worked and I bought cokes on hot days. She always looked sad. Gazed off into space. She had large oval shaped brown eyes and curly black hair. Her colourful skirts swished when she walked, like a Spanish woman, a real *mestiza*! Such a girl would have a hard time living without a man. As for the age difference, it didn't matter. She had grown to depend on Victor. He wasn't jealous, just protective. Everyone knows that the fellow in the bar, that night, was drunk and making obscene gestures. Remelita was scared and Victor, like any good husband, came to her rescue."

"Nonsense," said Rita. "You make her sound like a helpless child. She was a wealthy independent woman in her own right."

"How so?" I said.

"She owned the sari store where Robert bought his cokes and ogled at her," said Rita.

"Yes, and that's all Julius wanted. Her money," Robert answered.

"You're both wrong," said Lorina. "I knew her better than any of you."

"Speak up, Lorina," I said.

Lorina

"Remelita's mother was a widow, very dependent on her brother. He owned the convenience store that Robert mentioned. When she was growing up, Remelita worked there, after school. He'd visit his sister on the weekends and help out with money to buy food. But he expected certain privileges for his trouble. Remelita was pregnant by him when she was only thirteen. She had an abortion in some rat infested clinic and nearly bled to death. That's why she's never had any children.

"Victor knew about it and married her a few years later. She probably didn't love him at the time. But it was better with him than with the uncle, or ending up on the streets. At first Victor was crazy about her. Brought her home chocolates and perfume every pay day. Then, he started drinking. I think he always had. Roughed her up a bit. She took it at first. I don't know why. Maybe, she thought it was a wife's duty. What God gives us in life, we must accept. She wore dark sunglasses to hide the bruises on her face.

"Julius knew her back then. He used to clean out the uncle's store after school to make money. That's when they got involved. Not sexually. They were friends. He belonged to one of those evangelical churches and I think he hoped she would be his first convert. He kept insisting she was a child of God and deserved a better life.

" 'God doesn't give us trials,' Julius would say. 'You're intelligent. You can turn your life around.'

"He must have made an impression, because she did change. She stopped cowering behind the counter when the uncle came to check up on things, and she put her hands on her hips, and stared at men straight in the eye when they would look her up and down like the fold-out in a Playboy magazine. Somehow, she got her uncle to change his will and leave her his sari store. He had only one son who had gone to work in Japan. Maybe her uncle felt guilty after what he had done to her. Maybe she blackmailed him, threatened to tell his wife and the whole village. He was considered to be a respectable man since he sat on the Roman Catholic church board and the town council. As for Julius, he'd been a good friend, helped her at a bad time. I think it's a stroke of luck that her husband got thrown in jail. A few years ago the uncle died in a car accident. She's got a life, now."

"Convenient," said Rita. "Some people think she fixed the brakes."

"Gossip," said Robert. "Nothing was ever proven."

"Our class is nearly over for today," I said. "We still don't know what the problem is. Do you think it's your job to get Victor and his wife back together?" I waited for Rita's answer.

"Oh, no, Ma'am. It's much worse than that. We're afraid that Victor will try to get revenge on Julius and his family. One of Julius' sisters is married to my brother and lately we've seen strange men roaming around my parents' compound. My poor father went to see the mayor about it but we don't trust him. He's been in politics too long. Too many rings on his fingers and his hair slicked down with pomade. We believe he's accepting bribes from Victor's thugs. The mayor only said, 'Do you have any enemies?' My father said, 'No.' But he doesn't know about Julius' affair with Remelita. We want Julius to go away, find work in another country, but I don't think he'll break up with her. What advice should I give him? How can I make him to go away?"

"Can't you tell the police?" I asked.

A few of the students snickered and then Robert explained, "Last spring my father-in-law was robbed. His wife was upstairs in the bedroom and had fallen asleep reading. But he was downstairs watching TV. Some hoodlum got in through a back door. Put a knife to his throat. They drank all of his best wine and took everything they could lay their hands on, including his stereo. He was horrified that his wife would wake up and come downstairs."

"And the police, did he call them after the robbers were gone?" I asked.

"Oh. They were already there, Ma'am," and the whole class laughed.

At this point, Rita was nearly in tears. The bell had rung for chapel. These people always want to give advice, I thought, but there never seems to be any answers. The class folded their notebooks and Rita rushed away before I could promise to come to some conclusion the next time we met. Because it was the school's anniversary and a holiday declared, we didn't meet again for a while.

Two weeks went by, and I was worried about the class presentations. Robert had warned me of the students' fear of losing face, about the need to give answers. That's so unwestern, I thought. How can I help them encourage their clients and parishioners to make their own decisions, if they think their job is to dispense advice? I tried to learn more about the culture in the school's dimly lit library, but most of the books were outdated, donated to a developing country's college long after they had outlived their usefulness. There were no texts on counselling from either a western or Filipino perspective.

I found an article on philosophy and thought it was written in the sixties, the author was Filipino. He said, "So many outside forces affect the life of the average Filipino, typhoons, corruption in high places, joblessness, that personal problems are met with passivity. '*Adpat lang natin sundid ang pag-ikot ng mundo upang maiwasan ang gulo,*' is a common saying. It means we should follow the turning of the world in order to avoid trouble."

Just before classes started again, I met Rita on the gravel path that led to the bookstore. To my surprise she was all smiles.

"I have good news," she said. "Victor is getting out of jail on good behavior and is in the process of buying Remelita's sari store if he will give her a divorce."

"Wonderful," I said. "Does that mean there are no more prowlers in your father's compound?"

"Not lately."

"What about Remelita? How will she support herself when she sells the store? She's the one who needs your help, your counselling, now."

"I don't think she'll have any trouble. She's so beautiful she could be a film star if she wanted."

"Seriously, how will she earn her living?" She'll come under the influence of some dominating man again, I thought.

"*Bahala na.*"

"What does that mean?"

"What will be will be."

I shook my head. "I'm afraid I'm not a very good teacher, Rita. Things are so different, here." We linked arms and continued down the path.

"You're the best, Ma'am," she said. "We've learned so much."

After I returned to Canada, I worried about the students I had come to know and love. What did they learn from me? Could they survive doing things their own way, dispensing advice and trying to find answers? When Rita's letter came on that frosty afternoon, as I sat curled by a blazing fire, my mind was put to rest.

Dear Ma'am,

I hope this letter finds you well and happy. Perhaps you might like to know what happened to some of us after graduation. I was assigned to a church in Dasmarinas, a small town not far from our college, and Victor came to me for counselling after he left prison. He was afraid he might start drinking and get into trouble again. I must have given him very good advice because we fell in love and married.

Victor decided not to buy the sari shop from Remelita. Instead, the mayor purchased it for quite a sum when he retired from politics. Some people say that she blackmailed him,

threatening to expose the bribes he took while in office. I don't think so. At any rate, she hit
a windfall and used the money to set up a home for street children.

   Robert went to a large church in Manila. But shortly after that his wife died in childbirth
and that made us all very sad. We must accept the trials of life. Now, the gossip is that he
is courting Remelita. She says she won't leave her home and the girls and boys who are in
such need. We'll see.

   Julius emigrated to Canada, thanks to an aunt who owns a hair dressing salon and was
able to sponsor him. Now, he works in a TV studio in Toronto with the producer of an evangelistic
hour.

   We lost track of Lorina after she graduated. "Sa gulong ng palad." Life is a wheel of fortune.

Carefully, I folded the letter and put it between the first two pages of
my photo album. The last group picture I had taken of the students held
my attention. They posed formally, shoulders thrown back, smiles. Tall and
straight, they clumped together like bamboo growing by the river.
Nothing, not rains, nor floods, nor high wind, uproots this tall tough grass,
it clings so fast to the black soil.

III
In the Dry Woods

The town does not exist
except where one black-haired tree slips
up like a drowned woman into the sky

Anne Sexton

The rain kept falling. At the edge of the lake, slender reeds and bushes lifted their wet branches like the arms of the drowning. The road to Fung Jim Chow's laundry was no longer a road but more like a trough of water from which donkeys and horses, tired from lifting their feet out of the muck, could drink. Their riders spurred them on to the ridge above the road, narrow track of rotting leaves.

It rained and rained and Reverend Anthony Naylor, the missionary from England, looked out over his little congregation on Sunday morning and said, "I've never seen so much rain, even in London in the spring." He made jokes about building an ark if it kept up.

Even when it stopped pouring, clouds shrouded the top of the hills and threatened imprisonment between the slate-laden sky above and the curtains of fog below. There was no escape from this gray purgatory.

The lake, surrounded by mountains, was deep and treacherous and prone to sudden and violent storms. It measured about thirty miles long and was divided into two sections by a large peninsula of rock. The largest settlement, the Foot, was at the southern end of the lake. By the early nineteen twenties there were a few permanent buildings clustered on the shore: two hotels which competed with each other for the rich tourists from England, a somewhat disorganized school, and a few stores dotted along the main street.

Across the lake and to the north, stood an isolated logging camp called Inlet Bay. It was accessible only by water, a four hour boat ride between the Foot and the camp. Anthony was in the process of building a church at Inlet Bay and in a few short months the community would see its first school.

As in most of the settlements in the area, the houses floated on the water. Little gable-roofed cabins made of sturdy two-by-fours were built on rafts so they could move easily from one lumbering site to another. On a sunny day a stranger coming upon the floating community would have thought he had found a mystical village, shimmering in the mist of the surrounding rain forest, a Camelot or Avalon. The houses were surrounded by a platform and were connected to the land by a wooden walkway. However, only yesterday in the worst of the storm, one of them floated away from its moorings because the guy lines were rusted and they broke. Some houses stood firmly on land: a grocery store, the two hotels, a post office and the Anglican Church.

Jim Chow, his shoulders rounded and frail, face wizened, carefully wrapped the clean shirts in newspapers as he prepared for delivery. He hoped he could borrow someone's rowboat since the road through the village was flooded and his parcel too heavy to balance on the handlebars of his bicycle, even if the way were passable. It was Thursday. In anticipation of a weekend in Vancouver, the loggers had given him their best clothes to be cleaned and pressed: trousers worn at the knees, shirts frayed at the cuffs, buttons missing which he had painstakingly sewn back on. He knew the clothing would be returned more worn than before, covered with vomit or blood, pockets or collars torn and dangling, holes out of the knees which he would patch again. But they always returned, their money gone.

He fumbled while trying to tie string around the last parcel. His fingers, usually quick, moved heavily, awkwardly, as if they wanted to undo the parcel and shake the dress and put it out on a clothes line in the sun, as Megan probably would have done if she were alive.

Edith Weatherstone had brought the frock to him. The bodice was blood stained, not badly, because the bullet had gone clean through Megan's temple and the blood had trickled down her neck and over her left shoulder on to the floor. They had found her before the blood had dried and caked.

"Shot herself," said Mrs. Weatherstone. Her voice, almost as deep as a man's broke. She knew it and tried to gain her composure by drumming her fingers impatiently on the counter.

"Who?" He had to look up at her because she was quite tall.

"Megan. Shot herself" Jim didn't respond, so the woman thinking he didn't understand put it another way. "She's dead." Jim blinked. He felt his Adam's apple jerk up and down in his throat and that was the only sign he made that he had heard the dreadful news. "Reverend Naylor wants her dressed in this to send her back to her mother. Funeral's in Victoria." Mrs. Weatherstone brandished the dress at him, shaking it in his face as if it was his fault. "Oh no," he said. He steadied himself against the counter.

"Are you all right? He wants it to be ready by tonight." She tossed the dress on the counter.

"So sorry," he said.

"Yes. We're all sorry." She wheeled about and with her back turned to him muttered, "Very sorry." Without putting on her umbrella, she went out into the pouring rain. That was the longest conversation they had ever had.

Edith Weatherstone had known Megan would never last in the woods. She knew it from the moment the train whistled its way into the Duncan station and the girl, holding her skirt against the wind with one hand and clutching the shaky rail with the other, descended onto the platform and looked about anxiously. As if no one would be there to meet their children's teacher, thought Edith.

Megan's clothes were fashionable: an emerald green skirt and jacket and black boots without a scuff or scratch on their polished surface. "We'll see which wears out more quickly, her or her fancy shoes," Edith said to some of her friends the next day.

"We're here," called Alfred Weatherstone, waving his hat and rushing over to pick up her bag. His wife watched him shake hands and waited until he brought the girl over for the introduction.

"Mrs. Weatherstone," he said, still smiling, and he touched Megan's elbow as if she needed to be led like a blind person.

"Welcome. I hope the trip wasn't too tiring." Edith did not extend her hand but played with the pearl buttons on her crisp, white blouse.

"Not at all," said the girl as she tucked a few stray red curls under her hat.

On the way back, along the rutted road to the Foot, Megan grew silent. Alfred's Model T Ford jerked its way painfully over pot holes and around rocks, the road twisting and turning through the row of cedars and fir trees which crowded the thoroughfare, as if they were giant spectators reaching and craning their necks to catch a glimpse of a parade. No other cars travelled by. Alfred was one of the few owners of an automobile.

Yes, Edith knew that first afternoon, as her husband rushed around to the other side of the car to open the door and help the girl down onto the running board and the street, that Miss Megan McPherson would never belong.

Jim delivered the parcel on time to Reverend Anthony Naylor. The young minister nodded, thanked Jim and asked him if he could pay him tomorrow.

"No pay."

"Yes." He frowned and pursed his lips. Jim noticed the young man was paler than usual. "Tomorrow. I'll pay you then."

The laundry man shook his head. "I want to do something for her, too."

"I understand. Megan was fond of you, Jim." Anthony was about to turn away when he remembered. "I cleared up her desk and glanced over some of her papers. She liked your poetry, your sayings. She wrote some of them in her journal." The young man's black eyes glistened as he talked about her journal.

"Megan was a friend to many people," said Jim quietly. He pulled his wet jacket around his shoulders and returned to the boat he had managed to borrow.

Anthony put the parcel of Megan's clothing on the kitchen table. A draft had come in from the open door. He poured himself a cup of tea, and sat down beside the warm stove and listened to the crackling of the wood and the beating of the rain on the roof. Early tomorrow morning, he would deliver the parcel to the Weatherstone's house, where the women would dress Megan before she was sent back to Victoria for the burial.

He too remembered the day Megan arrived at the Foot. Mrs. Weatherstone was very anxious to get their new teacher to Inlet Camp that evening. Summer nights were long enough for travelling but a squall had come up over the lake and Anthony and Alfred insisted that Megan be allowed to stay at the Lakeside Hotel for the night.

"You must be tired," said Anthony to Megan. She assured him she was not and then stifled a yawn with a gloved hand.

"It's a long trip," said Mr. Weatherstone.

"Don't you want to get settled?" asked Edith.

"We'll get you room," said the priest.

"We can stay at your sister's," said Alfred to his wife.

"But she wants to unpack. We should take her to the camp now. So she can get organized," said Mrs. Weatherstone.

"No, she's exhausted."

"Are you hungry? Then it's settled. You must have some dinner," said Anthony as he led her away.

"She's got you eating out of her hand. She's got both of you at sixes and sevens," muttered Mrs. Weatherstone as Alfred told her to hush and took her arm.

"Now, now, dear. Let's go."

Anthony could still taste what they ate that night: delicious beef and kidney pie, the specialty of the house. Thick slices of fresh bread with butter melting into the crust and hot coffee and to top it all off berry pie cooked in sugar and cinnamon.

Megan ate quickly. Not like a bird pecking here and there at her plate, as the girls did back home in London. She ate in large gulps, little pyramids of carrots and potatoes piled perilously on her fork, some of it spilling into her lap. An embarrassed giggle.

"Taste good?" he said. She nodded. "Hotel's known for its food. Lots of tourists from England come here."

"Yes. They call it a hunter's paradise back in Victoria."

Queen Victoria's son came to fish years ago. Lots of nobility. They travelled by stage from Duncan and the Kowutzan guides took them back home down the river in their canoes."

She looked to him like a duchess or a princess, sitting upright in the straight backed chair. He wondered what had brought her here. He was aware that new graduates of normal school were sent to rural areas in order to try out their wings, but this girl? In a rough lumber camp at Inlet Bay?

"It must have been quite an adventure," she said.

"Do you like fishing?"

"No."

"Me neither. But there's nothing else to do here."

When Anthony had first arrived, the matrons gathered about the new missionary from England and tried to find him a suitable wife. "My niece from Nanaimo is coming for Christmas. Won't you join us for supper one night?" or "The next time you go into Victoria, drop in to my cousin's place and I'm sure you'd enjoy..."

But when the niece came or Christmas from Nanaimo she had just become engaged to a young banker in Toronto and the cousin's daughter was only sixteen and had buck teeth.

"What do you like to do? Your spare time. How do you spend it when you're not preparing lessons?" asked Anthony.

"Reading, I suppose." Then she told him about the collection of books she had brought. Before the evening was through, he had borrowed a novel by Katherine Mansfield and a collection of Shelley's poetry.

Someone was pounding at the door. Anthony, nearly asleep by the warm fire, jumped and then recognized Dan's voice. Too tired, he nearly didn't answer. More outpouring of grief, he thought. What about my feelings? Grumbling to himself, he got up from his comfortable chair and opened the door. There stood Dan, a faller who worked in the woods, but more importantly, Megan's fiancé.

"Didn't know if I should come in. Been drinkin'."

Beside the young missionary, Dan looked like Goliath before David.

"It's okay, Dan. Come in."

"Want some?" He held up a crock of home brew. Bootleggers thrived in the area. Rat-faced Ronnie, a man with a broken nose and one cheek bone smashed and now higher than the other due to a fight he'd lost years ago, was the camp's man supplier. He sold hooch by the glass but never washed the glasses. "So, where is she?"

"Megan? At the Weatherstone's. They're dressing the body tomorrow." Anthony said, "the body" because he wasn't sure Dan was facing reality. Even after Dan had seen Megan dead, he kept talking about her as if she were still alive. He had gathered the limp body up in his arms and cried out, "Don't leave me."

"Taking her back to Victoria?"

"Yes."

"Can't go in this weather."

"I know."

Anthony never understood what Megan had seen in Dan. This man, a logger, smelling of sweat and beer, standing in front of him in his dungarees and calk boots.

The priest still hadn't lived down the joke that some of the other loggers had played on him. Like everyone else, Anthony lived on a floathouse moored close to the land and connected to it my planks. Each year, he went back to Victoria to make his annual report to the bishop. While he was gone, some of the men from the Foot untied his dwelling and moved it to the brothel. All that week his house idled in the moonlight and the morning mist, drifted and swayed like an indolent boy, giddy with his first taste of brandy. Many times before this incident Anthony had watched the men trying to maneuver their way down the plank to the land in order to relieve themselves, had seen them fall into the water and had dragged them out, coughing and cussing before they nearly drowned. Did people think he was like that, capable of rutting and sweating and vomiting? He didn't realize that the same trick had been done to other priests at other times, that it was almost an initiation rite. Mrs. Weatherstone had refused to attend Bible Study until the matter was cleared up. Finally, Megan convinced Dan to help him move the house back to its usual spot.

"Just a joke. It's a tradition," he said. "We do it to every priest."

Later, Anthony realized he should have told Dan then, that the location of his float house wasn't the only subject of gossip and that people were beginning to talk about Dan and Megan, too.

Anthony poured his visitor a strong cup of tea. "Here, you need this."

"Want to hear my confession, Padre?"

"I did it. I killed her."

▲▼▲▼▲

If she stood on tip-toe on a rock, craning her neck like the heron when he looks for fish, Slemi could just see, over the window ledge, Megan's body stretched out, hands folded across her chest, blue skirt flowing down over the kitchen table. They had dressed her there because it was easier to wash the body and slit the back of her clothing with one of the kitchen knives in order to get her into it. Rigor mortis had set in by the time Anthony Naylor had delivered her funeral garb, a blue frock she wore only on Sundays.

The Indian girl and her brother were the only "natives" who attended the school. Their father was a trapper and they lived at the edge of the camp. Slemi peeked through the window. She hardly recognized her teacher. The red curls, usually impatiently thrust back behind her ears, were now pinned tightly in a bun at the nape of her neck. Her cheeks were as white as a clam shell, and her fingers, interlocked over the white buttons of her bodice, were as fragile as bird eggs, as pale as the blue winter sky.

Slemi remembered how her grandfather had looked on his death bed, his face painted soot black and ochre red, vibrant even though his spirit had fled. But what bothered Slemi most was the silence. The people moving about Megan sang no dirges, no wailing or plaintive chants sent her spirit into the sky, only silence and the relentless rhythm of the rain on the roof as if a ghost drummer filled the gray morning with empty sounds, waiting for masked ghost dancers who would stamp their feet and shake off sorrow.

Slemi watched Mrs. Weatherstone struggle to put a bonnet on Megan's head and tie the satin bow under her chin. The girl wished her grandfather were still alive and could summon the shaman in order to wake Megan because in the old days the medicine man could call back the spirit of the dead.

Mrs. Weatherstone, having finished the last of her meticulous duties, stood, hands on hips, and shook her head. Slemi didn't like Mrs. Weatherstone. She had overheard the older woman talking about Megan, how the new teacher couldn't keep order in her class, how she sometimes forgot to take the children outside to stand in a circle while one of them raised the flag or she left it flying in the breeze at the end of the day until it became tattered and faded and in one bad storm ripped nearly in two. Megan, so intent on telling the children stories or listening to theirs, forgot about flags and marches and taking partners and single file lines. She let the children burst out of the school into the sunshine or rain like a flock of noisy ducks, and she never used the hickory stick.

"How many of you know the story of Noah's flood?" she had said. That day they lined up by twos, two wolves, two elk, two bears. "And what are you?" she had said to Slemi

"An eagle," and she raised her arms and pretended to fly, darting among the children who neighed or barked or growled and that's when Mrs. Weatherstone appeared, hands on hips. After she had gone, Slemi told Megan her own story about when the rains came an the children sat quietly pretending they were on a raft in the middle of the flood near Mount Tzouhalem. The Indian girl told the class how a young man and woman had been chosen by the tribe to save the children and how it rained days and nights and all the adults died—just as in the Noah story. Megan had listened and Slemi told her how a sea otter swam by with a salmon in his mouth and tossed it onto the raft and how he fed the children until the waters receded and they could return to dry land. Then the class drew pictures in their scribblers of the animals in both legends. Slemi fashioned the dove that flew back to the ark with a leaf in his mouth and then soared away again, never to return. She wished her bird had come alive and she could have caught it in her hands and skinned it and made a magic cape so that Megan could have flown away from grim Mrs. Weatherstone.

Fung Jim Chow came to pay his respects. Since he wasn't sure he would be welcome he brought an armload of laundry, Mr. Weatherstone's shirts, pressed and smelling sweet of balsam soap. He did not know if he would be considered one of them, one of the mourners, because the only social interchange he had with the residents at the camp was at Christmas when he brought lychee nuts and a tin of ginger, neatly wrapped in paper and tied with a red ribbon, a pine cone or a bit of cedar delicately set between the loops.

He had come to Canada in his early twenties in the hopes of acquiring enough wealth so that he could return to China a rich man. There was a girl back home. He worked on the railroad. His last job in a section gang was the seventeen miles between Duncan and the Foot. It opened in 1913 not for passengers but for the transport of logs to the mills. Gradually he realized that he would never go back home, that the girl he dreamed about had probably married someone else. The years went by and he bore the cold winters, the hunger, the loneliness until he caught influenza. His body could no longer take the rigors of outdoor work and so with the little money he saved he established a laundry.

Megan was the only one who had invited him into her house and at Christmas given him a present, a pair of mittens she had knit in soft green yarn. He had come upon her standing at the river's edge so lost in thought that when he approached she jumped. When she turned around he saw that her eyes were red because she had been crying.

"Alone?" he said.

"Yes. It's okay. Dan's over at the hotel. At the shooting contest."

"Guns. Too noisy."

"Yes. Well, I have some of the children's work still to mark."

"Work? Christmas day?"

"Yes. I have to. Some of the parents have complained…"

"Me too, A wrinkle here, a mark there on this shirt, on this dress."

"They're fussy." She smiled and turned back to stare into the water. He stood beside her in silence. The river swished by like a giant runaway bolt of silk, tumbling off a giant tailor's shelf, falling and uncurling in sprays of foam, pearl seeds unglued. Ducks in single file swam in perfect formation against the current, then, as if to provide comic relief, turned upside down so that even the white tuft of their tails disappeared under the water. She wasn't looking at them but gazed into the swirling depths as if she were trying to see her own reflection.

"Isn't it terrible being so far away from home?" she asked.

"At first, I was lonely. But I remembered the teachings of my grandfather. They gave me peace."

"Would you teach them to me, too?"

"If you would like to learn from an old Chinese laundry man," he smiled.

"Yes. I want peace of mind," she said. "But first, I'll give you your Christmas present," He followed her into the house. Before he left, he had told her some of the sayings of his father and she had written them in a thick journal.

Learning to meditate:

When by the side of the ancient ferry, the breeze and moonlight are cool and pure, the dark vessel turns into a glowing world.

When Megan had arrived at the camp, she lived in the schoolhouse in a room no bigger than a cupboard. But Alfred and some of the loggers said it wasn't good enough and they built her a house, not a floathouse but a cabin on land. That was how she met Dan, since he was one of the first men to chop down the trees and hammer the logs together row on row. After that people started talking about them because they were so often seen together. People gossiped in front of Jim as if they thought he was deaf, so sure he couldn't understand or perhaps didn't have natural feelings like other men or that he didn't matter.

"They aren't even engaged!" said Mrs. Weatherstone.

"She had him for dinner Sunday night," said the storekeeper's wife.

"Did you see him leave?" queried a young woman holding her baby.

"Did she go to Victoria, see her mother on the same weekend that he went into town?" asked Mrs. Weatherstone.

Jim Chow rapped gently on the Weatherstone's door, and held out his parcel of laundry. Anthony Naylor motioned to him.

"Come in. The women just finished dressing her."

Megan's skin, pale and translucent, stretched tight over the high cheekbones. Her eyes were closed, lids fine as silk, almost transparent, hiding eyes that used to dart like minnows in the shallow part of the river. Her pale lips upturned at the corners, almost smiling. She looked as if she was contemplating. Was she at last at peace, at one with the Tao?

More than once Jim had come upon Megan staring into the river, or sitting down by the lake. At first he only nodded but gradually he began to realize that she didn't mind his company, even expected it. He would put down his parcel of laundry on a rock, or squat beside her and watch the heron fish. He saw her moods change like the water: on one day calm reflecting the sun, on another whipped up by wind. Sometimes she seemed heavy, like the river in spring swollen with run-off and rain, water brimming over the edge of the bank, flooding the tender reeds and spring shoots as a woman's tears on a pillow.

Once he had come upon her reading and asked what it was she wanted to understand.

"Blake," she had said. "A nineteenth-century poet."

"Read out loud," he said.

"*To see the world in a grain of sand*
   and heaven in a wild flower
   hold infinity in the palm of your hand
   and eternity in an hour."

"And now a Chinese poem by Hung-chih Cheng-chio." Then he recited.

"*The white bird disappears in vapor; the autumn stream unites in heaven.*"

"Your poems don't rhyme?" She asked, frowning.

He smiled at her and instead of answering the question he rested his hand lightly on her shoulder. "My father said that all things go to the source. All things come from it."

"What is the source?' she asked.

"Tao."

"What is the Tao?'

"In the dry woods a dragon is singing," he said as he rose to his feet.

"They're beautiful poems," she said. "Is the dragon God?"

Before he could answer, she picked up her diary and began writing.

Dan watched the laundry man, thin and emaciated, bow to Megan and go as he had come, like a shadow. For a moment he thought he saw her breasts rise and fall slightly, as if she were taking a little breath.

"Have some coffee, some scones?" said Mrs. Weatherstone.

"No."

"Haven't you eaten today? She'd want you to take care of yourself, Dan."

"It was she who took care of me."

"Yes. And she'd want you to go on living."

"I wish I had died."

On the day of Dan's accident the women had listened as they always did for the sound of the whistle. They heard its sharp ring above the screeching of birds, the barking of dogs. They waited for the short whistle blasts and counted. One, two, three, four, five. The children stopped playing. Six blasts meant an accident. Eight a death. On that day the women counted six. They scrambled into their coats and rushed out of their houses. The older wives embraced the younger ones. Each woman turned and looked at the other, "Is it my husband or yours?"

When Dan first went into the woods, he worked with an experienced faller and learned to gauge the descent of the hill and how the tree would fall. Now he was considered by the other loggers to be such a careful man that the younger boys worked with him. No one expected that day that the tree would crash against a snag with such force that the dying tree hidden in the underbrush would flip into the air and strike him on the head even as he ran. The first aid came as quickly as he could and got Dan into the boat. At the other side of the lake they piled into Alfred Weatherstone's car but they were delayed by the tortuous road full of pot holes and sharp twists. By the time Dan arrived in Duncan he was in a state of shock and nearly dead.

Oct. 3, 1923

Dear Editor

I am writing on behalf of the settlement at the Foot, Inlet Bay and loggers and their families in other camps around the lake. We request that a hospital be built. It is my understanding that two deaths occurred in the woods last year simply because medical help was not immediately available. Messrs. Anderson and Bergren could have been saved but the former bled to death and the latter, who suffered severe burns to his body, died at the front doors of the King's Daughter's Hospital. Furthermore, our communities are growing. Mothers-to-be must go to Duncan days or weeks before their confinement and our children, when they are sick, are also at risk. Lack of proper medical facilities is a shameful mark against the timber companies for disrespect for their own workers.

Sincerely yours,
Megan McPherson

Perhaps that is what made some of the people so angry, not Megan's shenanigans with Dan but her meddling in affairs that went far beyond her students and the school. That's what Anthony thought as he watched Dan stroke her hand and refuse Mrs. Weatherstone's tea and scones.

Megan had stayed after church one day. "Anthony, we have to do something about the way the men live. Do you realize they only get one blanket and their cots are infested with bedbugs and lice?"

"Yes. It's a hard life." The priest had gone to what the men called the bull pens, the bunkhouses, and warmed his hands at the stove in the middle of the room He had shared their heavy diet of bacon and beans and rice, and if they were lucky, a few prunes. "They used to call the loggers bindle-stiffs because they carried their blanket rolls from camp to camp."

"Something should be done," she said. That's when the spate of letters began.

▲▼▲▼▲

Anthony had planned to send Megan's body back to Victoria for burial on the speeder but, with the torrential downpour, the tracks were buried in mud and the self-propelled railroad car was out of commission.

Slemi came to pay her respects more than once, not only to hover about her teacher, but also to taste Mrs. Weatherstone's berry tarts and sugar cookies.

"Miss McPherson was very fond of you, Slemi."

"Yes," she said wiping the crumbs from her mouth.

"She liked your stories."

"I liked hers, too."

Anthony had gathered up Megan's personal possessions and planned to give them to her mother in Victoria. In rummaging through her desk he found a journal she had been keeping. He put aside his discomfort at reading her secrets. It was a way of knowing her better, making sense of her death. Apparently one of Megan's favourite legends was about the Stonehead people.

Slemi told me the story of the chief's daughter, the child of a favourite slave, a beautiful woman of the northern tribes. Their daughter was even more beautiful than her mother and many warriors sought her hand in marriage. Instead of choosing one of the Stonehead braves, she fell in love with a Comiakin warrior. Eventually the chief consented to the marriage with the understanding that his daughter would not leave home. All was well until the old man died. No longer under the chief's protection, the Comiakin brave was brutally murdered by his wife's former jealous suitors. The young widow, pregnant and fearing for her life, fled into the forest where she gave birth.

I must tell Slemi the story of Hagar and how she fled into the desert with her son. They both survived and she became the mother of great men. I suppose I shall survive too, here in this wilderness.

Anthony became aware of Slemi leaning into him. She whispered in his ear, "Miss McPherson nearly died once before. Stinqua got her."

"What are you talking about?"

Slemi told him about the first time she had seen the lake monster. She and her grandfather had spent the morning fishing when a squall developed. Her grandfather had pulled their canoe up onto the beach while the water in the deep part of the lake churned and eddied with the thrashing of Stinqua's tail. They could see the hump of his back, his mouth open, teeth glistening in the foam. Last spring, the monster destroyed the weir at the mouth of the river where the Nitinaht speared salmon, swimming upstream. A few years before, he overturned and gulped a whole canoe and its passengers.

Anthony half believed in the legend, himself. Sudden storms churned up the lake with no warning and both the loggers and the natives believed the white foam was caused from the slashing of the great tail of the fish.

Megan had told Slemi's class that there was only one sea monster who had swallowed a man whole and that was in the Bible. "Jonah lived in the whale's stomach for three days. Then he was coughed up onto the land," the teacher explained.

"Wait. He'll come after you, too," warned Slemi.

"I'm not afraid," said Megan. "No monster's going to eat me."

But he nearly did. Winter came early. The trees, stiff with ice, looked like white phantoms in the mist. The snow came down thick as feathers and everyone thought the lake had frozen solid because the men had to saw the ice from around the floathouses. Slemi saw Megan talking to a stranger in a red hat at the far side of the platform. What was she doing over there, away from everyone? He seemed angry and Slemi drew closer to listen. Then Megan lost her balance, or had he pushed her? Slemi yelled for help, sharp high pitched yelps. She could see Megan's red head bobbing up and down in the froth like a duck plunging into the water then riding back up to the surface only to dive under again. The man in the red cap lay down on his stomach and reached out for her hand thrashing wildly in the cold air. She went down again and Slemi thought for a minute he had pushed her under but then she realized Stinqua had Megan's feet in his teeth.

Dan appeared and the man grabbed his red hat and slipped around the back of the house, across the platform and up the hill. By this time Dan had Megan by the arms and was pulling her out of the mouth of the monster.

They took her to Mrs. Weatherstone's house and Slemi ran ahead with news that her teacher had fallen into the lake.

Mrs. Weatherstone wrapped Megan in blankets and gave her hot tea. "Leave it alone," said Alfred. "It's not your business."

Slemi thought he meant the lake monster.

"But it is my business. I care about those men. Dan's one of them. Maybe a son of mine will go into the woods one day."

"Look, those letters don't do any good. You'll just get hurt. You say that man pushed you under?"

"He said, 'Keep your mouth shut.' Before I knew it I was under the water. If Dan hadn't come…"

"Scare tactics," said Dan.

"Ever see him before?" said Alfred.

"My grandfather and I saw him. Swallowed a whole canoe," said Slemi.

"Shh. Now you go home. That's a good girl." Mrs. Weatherstone led her to the door.

"I may have seen him around camp. I guess I thought he was a trapper, or a remittance man."

Slemi couldn't stop talking about it. She told her mother how Stinqua had caught Megan by the foot and if Dan hadn't come would have pulled her into the lake.

"Will he try again?" said Slemi.

"He's very angry," said her mother. "But he shouldn't go after the teacher."

Her mother talked softly and with no bitterness and she looked away from Slemi to the scarred hills, to the bare patches, blank open spaces, where no trees stood, no birds flew, no animals tended their young, where the slash lay, fallen trees, naked bodies, pale and white from lying in the sun. Only the wind whipped and moaned over the desecrated land like a crazed girl seeking her dead love.

Anthony Green told Megan not to leave it alone. He offered to help.

"We can get them to sign a petition on Sunday. The whole congregation."

"Are you sure? I don't want you getting into any trouble. What will the bishop think?"

"Didn't Jesus say, 'When I was sick did you visit me and when I was in prison…?'"

"Yes. But this is different. There's politics involved."

"Social action. Ever hear of it? Wouldn't Jesus have cared if he had seen how the men live? And you too, Megan. It's not an easy life out here in the woods."

He wanted to take her hand and hold it in his, touch the white skin before it became rough and red and weatherworn like the other women's. He wanted to smooth back the red curls from her face and kiss her wide, strong forehead, her stubborn chin, her lips.

Instead he said, "Why did you come? Why didn't you stay in the city?"

"Work," she shrugged. "I want to be independent."

Anthony wished he had gotten a good look at the man with the red cap because he was convinced Megan's death wasn't suicide. Her letters to the newspapers and the lumber company had made enemies. A few years ago a union had been formed to improve the loggers' working conditions. But in a couple of years it fell apart. It was rumoured that some of the leaders had absconded with the funds. Even though anyone who demanded better working conditions was branded as a Communist, he knew it would be just a matter of time before there was another union formed.

The church council wouldn't allow the petition Anthony had promised Megan but nothing could stop him from preaching in the style of the great prophets. "Let judgment roll down as waters, and righteousness as a mighty stream."

When Anthony was a boy, his mother had hung on his bedroom wall a needlepoint picture of Jesus as a pensive young man, carrying a lamb in his arms. She had nursed him on such Bible verses such as " A soft word turneth away wrath." But the scene that inspired Anthony to be ordained was of his own creation, a picture in his imagination of Jesus driving the money changers out of the temple, brandishing a whip, overturning chairs, shouting. He relished a vision of the son of God as a rebel, breaking the Sabbath, consorting with tax collectors and fallen women, confronting the Scribes and Pharisees, the conservatives of his day.

When Anthony had first arrived in the Cowichan Valley, he thought with God's help he could make a difference. Men who came to his church would stop drinking. The wives of his congregation would not be bullied or struck by their husbands. Gradually, he realized he had little power and that all he could do was comfort and love his flock. He could give a vagrant a decent meal, let a man cry when his son drowned, or tell a homesick bride her cake was the best he had ever tasted. Then Megan arrived with her red hair and books, her letters and her proud dreams of a new hospital.

After Slemi had eaten her second sugar cookie, Anthony said he would walk her home. On the way, she told him about Stinqua, the monster in the lake. He didn't shake his head as Megan had done but he listened to her stories of storms and overturned canoes and whole families devoured in one gulp. He had seen enough pain and suffering, greed and cruelty to begin to believe in a power of evil.

"Yes. He's out there," said the young priest. He took Slemi's hand and they stood for a long time, searching the lake, calm in the afternoon sunlight, watching for a sign of the leviathan.

▲▼▲▼▲

The sun shone for a couple of hours the day they loaded Megan's coffin on the train. Dan saw the break in the weather as a sign that she had forgiven him, that the pale yellow beams, slender as fingers, were her hand extended in a heavenly benediction.

After all, she had seen him drunk before, had steadied him when he walked the plank to her floathouse, had made coffee and pulled off his boots, had covered him up with her own quilt made of unmatched squares. The sky with the hole in it looked like her blanket, one of the patches torn loose. He half-wished to be covered in its gray, soft folds.

On that last night, they had gone to a party in the community hall. Like the other buildings, it floated in the curve of the bay in the middle of the yellow water lilies. He made her dance. She pushed him away as the floor dipped and the floathouse tipped, the dancers having moved to the far end in a huddle of sweat and foot stomping. Anthony stopped the fiddlers twice and directed the melée of boots and high-heeled shoes to the centre of the floor. Still, it veered this way and that.

"I don't want to dance. Not tonight." said Megan.

"I'll hold you. You won't slip and fall."

"No, I don't feel like dancing."

Then suddenly he lost his balance and his own boots were up in the air. Anthony's face was over his.

"Let her be."

Back on his feet Dan lunged at the priest and hit him a good one on the jaw.

"Find your own girl."

"I'm going home," said Megan and Dan followed her out the door.

They had gone back to her place, arm in arm, she supporting him, he breaking into a skip, slipping in the mud, hopping, grabbing her around the waist and swirling about in a mock waltz, steadying her pliant body against his and finally making her laugh.

The wind had suddenly whipped up and their faces in the rain were wet and cold. "In the spring, we'll be married," he promised. He had said it to her before, as if their marriage would bring the sunshine, but each time she shook her head.

"No, Dan. You're too much like my Dad."

He'd heard that before, too. Megan's father's drinking had lost him one job after another, and they had moved from house to house, sometimes in the middle of the night. Megan had promised herself then, when she was just a child, that she would never depend on any man.

"I'm a teacher, Dan. I'll take care of myself."

Dan moved log jams. He poked and pushed and cajoled the massive trunks until he got his way. This one moved a foot or two and thudded against that one. Gradually they succumbed to his will and glided on down the river.

"I'll take care of you, Megan. You'll never go hungry with me." He tried to put his arm around her and ease her down on the bed.

"I can fish." He wanted to show her his new rod. To lay it on the bed like a wedding gift. "I can hunt, " he said.

She kept a rifle in the closet. He wanted to lay that down on her cot too, let her run her fingers over the barrel and then watch him get up, go to the open door, take aim and shoot something, a bird, a raccoon, anything that moved in the night. He wanted to offer it up like a wedding gift, lay a trophy down on the pillow for her to admire.

"What are you doing?" she said.

"Showing you something."

"Give me the gun."

"Marry me." He put his arm around her to steer her towards the bed and gently ease her down beside his gifts that he imagined lay in profusion on the quilt.

"Give it to me." She pushed him away as she had done on the dance floor and he remembered Anthony's face cutting in between them.

"You love somebody else."

"I love you. But I hate it when you get drunk."

"It's Anthony Naylor. You're going to be the vicar's wife."

"Stop it. Leave me alone."

He didn't know if she was pushing him away or grabbing for the gun.

He remembers slapping her. He doesn't know how many times. He hopes only once. The gun lay beside her when she was found the next morning. He doesn't remember leaving, or making love, or anything after that first smack across her face, the crack of his hand against her jaw, or was it the rap of the bullet after he had pulled the trigger? Click, smack, bang.

He couldn't remember.

Anthony said a brief prayer when Dan and Alfred had loaded the coffin on the train. "Blessed are they which die in the Lord. The souls of the righteous are in the hands of God. There shall no torment touch them."

Clouds closed over the blue rift in the sky through which the sun had shone for a few hours. They poured their tears over those few who came to pay their respects to Megan before she sped home to her mother in Victoria. The sky wept, as though it was exhausted, having vented its grief over the land ever since the morning her body had been found. At first the rain shielded the mourners from each other, gave them privacy under umbrellas and wide-brimmed hats. Then it became a shower, a gentle pit-a-pat, singing Megan to her eternal rest.

Anthony closed his prayer book while the engine cranked and wheezed. He stared down at its worn back leather jacket and thought about what Megan had written in her journal. It was about him, Anthony.

There was another tragedy in the woods yesterday. A high rigger fell to his death. I don't think our priest believes in the almighty God any more. Anthony wishes he could do more for his parishioners, improve their working conditions somehow. He reminds me of Jesus when our Lord wept over Jerusalem. I believe God weeps for us too.

Alfred took off his hat and shook the water from its brim. "Come for a coffee?" he said to Dan.

"No. Gotta pack up."

"Leaving? Where?"

"Don't know. Not going back into the woods again."

"What will you do?"

Dan shrugged his shoulders.

"If it wasn't for that damn letter," said Alfred.

"What letter?" asked Dan.

"Didn't she tell you?"

"No. Had an argument."

Alfred had wanted to tear the letter to pieces. He had received a similar missive years ago about Edith. His father had not wanted him to marry her as there was some disgrace in the family. His wife's sister had a child by a married man, a lord or someone from England who had been looking at buying property, setting up a hunting lodge. Alfred hadn't listened to the details of the story, he had been so in love, so set on marrying a woman of his own choice. The girl had gone into service back east and the family lost track of her. Probably died in childbirth, he thought. He married regardless of his father's criticisms. Over the years his wife had changed. Once spontaneous, daring and pretty, she had become self-righteous, religious, jealous. When other women became round with maturity, soft and more giving, Edith grew thin, her elbows and thighs sharp with protruding bones, her breasts not pendulous and nurturing with age, but small and flat.

> *The board regrets advising you that there have been certain allegations regarding your conduct in the classroom.*

Certain allegations, certain stiff-necked thin lipped matrons that had nothing more to do than gossip.

> *The complaints being the following:*
>
> *1. On Sept 23, and Oct. 8 the flag was left flying and had to be lowered by Mr. Weatherstone in the evening as on both nights there was a storm.*
>
> *2. The children's notebooks are wasted with drawings and doodlings rather than writing and arithmetic.*
>
> *3. There have been reports of unruly classroom behaviour.*

Yes, and reports too of a man seen leaving Megan's house before dawn, he thought.

> *and that unless there is considerable improvement, the contract will not be extended into the next year.*

Alfred had tried to comfort Megan at the dance that night. Dan had left her alone for a moment to get drinks, and Edith was chatting with some women.

"You're out of sorts, Megan, not your usual spirited self tonight." He sat beside her. "Is it the letter? Mustn't take it all so seriously."

"They've shamed me," she said. "Criticizing me at the breakfast table. Talking about me at dinner. Keeping track of me. Writing complaints. In front of my own pupils."

"The children love you," he said.

"They'll laugh at me now. Every time I turn my back. And what if I can't find another placement?"

"Oh Megan. You're not fired. Just a warning."

"But they will fire me. I'm ruined." She began to cry. "Excuse me, sir." She got up and hurried away leaving him sitting alone.

Mrs. Weatherstone heard first about the train derailment. She had the camp's only telephone.

"New roadbed's too soft," said the engineer. "Too much rain. She just rolled over into the lake."

"The coffin? Is it safe?"

"Near floated away."

"But is she safe?"

"The train? She'll make it. Another engines on its way with block tackle and lines."

"No, no. The coffin. The body."

I never wanted harm to come to Megan but surely this ignominious end is some kind of divine retribution, she thought as she hung up the phone.

"The girl has no standards," she had complained to Alfred one night at dinner. "Does she think we don't notice what's going on? Dan leaving her place in the middle of the night. Trips to Victoria?"

"They'll be married in the spring. Hold your tongue."

"No, she's refused him. At least she's showing a bit of intelligence."

"He's a good lad. Works hard. He's good to her."

"He's a drunk and she's a tart and I won't have the likes of her influencing the children."

It only took a few meetings of like-minded women, and a few men (most of them were reluctant to point a finger at the prettiest girl in the camp) to write a letter of complaint to the superintendent. Alfred had delivered it against his will.

Megan had been drawing water from the well, her back turned to him. She was singing softly to herself.

"Something for you," he said, brandishing the paper in front of him as if it was contaminated.

"Will you come in for a cup of tea?"

"No, no. Lots of errands." He didn't want to watch her open it.

When the second engine arrived, the men hooked it up to the one that had overturned. For hours in the rain, they pulled and strained the cables and then, slowly, the second engine rolled over in the opposite direction and fell into the rising water around the shore of the lake.

Anthony Naylor helped Alfred carry the coffin back home, but this time Megan rested in the barn.

"Poor thing, I didn't expect it to come to this," said Mrs. Weatherstone as she pulled at the wet sleeves of her husband's dripping coat and hung it on a hook.

"We should have stood by her more. Not criticized so much. It was only her first year teaching," he said.

"Are you still blaming yourself? You think she killed herself because of our complaints!" gasped Edith.

"The letter shamed her," he muttered not wanting to look at Edith's face flushing with anger.

"The letter? She was pregnant. Everyone knows that but you."

▲▼▲▼▲

Jim Chow watched the men struggle with the coffin. Slipping in the mud, they opened the barn door and set their burden carefully down.

"She should have left it alone. Writing to the papers. Getting people stirred up," said Alfred. He took off his hat and shook the water off it.

"It was my fault. I encouraged her," said Anthony.

"Someone tried to drown her once. Remember? That day the lake was frozen and we had to cut away the ice. Why did you take her to those damn meetings?"

"Unions are forming all over. Farmers, coal miners. Loggers aren't organized, yet but we thought, I thought…"

"She had no business meddling." Alfred set his hat firmly on his head and the two men walked back out into the rain.

When they had gone, Jim Chow slipped into the barn and squatted beside the coffin. He didn't notice Slemi crouched in the corner. She was not sure she should be there at all. Used to being shooed away, she kept still. After the arguing of the two men, the shelter was quiet but when the laundry man sat like a statue in front of the coffin an even greater hush settled over the shed. It was not yet evening. For a moment Slemi thought he had fallen asleep but his eyes were open.

He was remembering the day Anthony had come with a bag of white shirts that needed to be pressed and cleaned. He hoisted the bundle on to the shelf and said, "I've got something else for you. Some poems Megan transcribed. I think they're yours. Listen."

"Jim Chow says I shouldn't worry so much about their criticism. I guess he knows what it's like to be shunned. We were sitting by the river and he said, "You asked me about success and failure. There is a Chinese saying, 'The fisherman's song goes deep into the river.' I wish I knew that song.

"You gave her comfort." Anthony's wet brown hair curled in wisps against his forehead and droplets of water had run down his neck and dampened the front of his shirt. Jim Chow handed him a towel. "It is Buddhist writing. Like your Bible."

"I'm afraid my Bible didn't give her much comfort. There's another entry here."

"Jim Chow says thoughts are like birds and I think too much. I was feeding some geese and we watched them fight for the few crumbs left on the ground. Here is another one of his verses: Boundless is the sky where flying birds disappear into the unseen."

After what seemed a long time, Jim Chow rose to his feet and, closing the door quietly behind him, he left the barn.

When he had gone, Slemi crept closer to her teacher's casket. The wood was wet and luminous, as if Megan's spirit, trapped inside, waiting to be free, lit the whole box. She sat with her arms clasped around her legs, her chin resting on her knees, dreaming about Megan.

A sparrow flew down from the rafters and perched on the coffin. "Have you come to visit me, little friend?" said Slemi. She extended her hand but the bird flew back to its hiding place.

Megan had told her a story about someone called Hagar who had been forced to run away with her child into the desert. "And she became a great woman," Megan had said. "She survived on her own, without anyone's care, not even her husband's."

Slemi knew that was not easy, that it was hard to be alone. She and her brother, the only "natives" in the school, had too often been called names, shoved into the dirt and left alone to amuse themselves while the others chose teams and played together.

She wasn't sure if Megan really believed what she taught about the importance of being independent. "One person cannot stand alone," Slemi's grandfather said.

Once the girl had followed her teacher into the woods and found Megan crying. Megan had flung her arms around a large tree trunk as if she wanted to be embraced and there she had fallen down onto the moss and wept loudly so that Slemi was almost afraid. Just as the young girl was about to come out of her hiding place, Dan came into the clearing. She couldn't hear what they said to each other but Megan threw her arms around him and he held her and covered her body with his. Slemi left them lying there, arms and legs entangled, the sun casting a gold light through the trees, transforming the lovers into glittering copper statues.

The sparrow flew down from his perch again and fluttered back and forth. This time it would not land on the coffin or her extended hand and she realized it was confused and trapped. She got up and opened the barn door and waited until he had found the light and freedom before she closed the door again and left Megan alone.

▲▼▲▼▲

Megan's mother gave Anthony permission to bury her daughter in the woods because the body was beginning to decompose. As soon as there was a break in the weather, a small circle of people gathered under a towering cedar covered in green moss. It shook its branches every now and then as if the heavens were casting holy water in a final blessing. They assembled in silence around the hole some of the loggers had prepared, and the coffin was lowered into the earth.

Slemi looked away as the men began to cover the casket over with soil and eventually she turned her back and watched the mist circling, a lost ghost in the timber. Her grandfather's box had been lifted high into the branches of a tree, not buried under ground away from the sun and wind. Before he died he had told her to look for him in the storm. "The thunder and lightning are a sign that our loved ones have not left us and are visiting the earth," he said.

Slemi looked up as the canopy of leaves parted in the rising wind, and she was sure she caught a glimpse of gathering thunderclouds.

Jim Chow was also among the mourners. He listened to the steady clump of wet earth as it fell on the casket. He remembered sitting with Megan by the lake and listening to a similar rhythm as the waves lapped against the rocks. He had found her alone, throwing stones into the cold water and studying the concentric circles that formed and moved out into the deeper part of the cove.

"They don't like me," she said.

"Who?"

"The other women. They gossip."

"Who do they like? Not me."

"I try to be nice. Please them…"

"No," Jim interrupted. "Listen."

That story too, she had recorded in her journal. Anthony had shown it too him. He hadn't let on to the young priest how surprised he had been that his sayings and tales had meant so much to her. Anthony had read it out loud.

> *"Once a Buddhist man went to visit the great master Ma-tsu. 'Why did you come here?' asked the teacher.*
>
> *"'To be enlightened.'*
>
> *"'Why did you leave your home and wander about and neglect your own precious treasure?' the master asked.*
>
> *"'What is my treasure?' said the visitor.*
>
> *"'It is he who has just asked the question. It contains everything and lacks nothing. There is no need to seek it outside yourself.'"*

Jim Chow remembered that Megan had stopped throwing stones into the lake. For a long time they sat wordlessly watching the water crest in a white froth against the rocks and fall away.

Anthony watched while the men covered Megan's coffin with shovelfuls of wet black soil. The rough wood reminded him of the cross. She died for a cause, for justice, he thought. He reached into his pocket and fingered a square of neatly folded paper. On her desk he had found some letters she had written, and fragments of poetry.

I shouldn't have encouraged her to write to the newspapers, he thought. How many enemies did she have? Who did she talk to without my knowledge? He tried to focus on the words he was about to say to comfort the group of mourners. I won't let her die in vain. Then standing over Megan's open grave he promised that a union for loggers would be formed. I'll make it happen, he promised.

When the men were finished he opened his prayer book and began the service. "I am the resurrection and the life, saith the Lord: he that believeth in me, though he were dead, yet shall he live: and whoever liveth and believeth in me shall never die."

Mrs. Weatherstone stood beside her husband, her back tall and straight, chin in the air. Unrepentant. Alfred, his arm linked in hers, frowned and cleared his throat periodically. Dan was there too, surrounded by loggers, uncomfortable in their clean Sunday clothes. Most of the children from the school were present. Clinging to their parents, they were the only ones who cried openly. Slemi stood apart from everyone, her back to the group. Jim Chow, usually distant and aloof, came as close to her grave and the little group of mourners as he dared.

Anthony paused for a moment and then said, "Before we end our service today I want to read to you two poems, one from the Bible and one that Megan wrote herself. She was a high-spirited person but to some of us who knew her well there was a dark side to her nature, a yearning and loneliness that was hard for some of us to understand. Those of us who loved her would like to think our affection gave her some comfort. The greatest solace I can offer you on this sad occasion is to say that none of us is ever completely alone. God's love and presence is always with us, in this life and the next. Listen to what Saint Paul said in the book of Romans, chapter eight, "*For I am persuaded, that neither death, nor life, nor angels, nor principalities, nor powers, nor things present, nor things to come, nor height, nor depth, nor any other creature, shall be able to separate us from the love of God, which is in Christ Jesus our Lord.*"

Anthony closed his prayer book and, pulling the poem out of his pocket, he explained to the mourners how he had found it in her journal. "I think she might want me to read this," he said.

"*In the dry woods*
a dragon is singing.
On his white breath
I would fly
into vapours of mist
away.
On that day
my shrivelled heart
will hear a woodsfull
of dragon songs.
Solitary, I sit among dry trees
and listen."

There were a few moments of silence broken only by the rustle of wet leaves and a muffled roll of thunder from somewhere in the east. "God grant her eternal rest," said Anthony. He raised his arms in a blessing and the crowd dispersed.

Acknowledgments

There are many people to thank for inspiring and coaching me as I wrote this collection of short stories. I owe a debt of gratitude to Candas Dorsey and the Books Collective for having enough faith in me to publish two of my books. Tim and Candas have offered respectful critique and friendship over the years.

I would like to thank Rudy Wiebe for allowing me to attend his Creative Writing evening classes when I lived in Edmonton. At that time, the writers in residence at the University of Alberta also helped me hone my craft.

In various communities, a circle of students, writers, parishioners, and friends have enriched my life and writing. While serving as the minister in Lake Cowichan United Church on Vancouver Island, I read Lynne Bowen's colourful book, *Those Lake People*. I was fascinated to learn about Mabel Jones who lived and taught at Camp Six on Lake Cowichan, British Columbia in the year 1928. Inspired by her tale of loneliness and desperation, I have fictionalized the account of her life and death and have written the story *In The Dry Woods*. Other books were helpful too. *When The Rains Came* by Turner was the source of some of the First Nations' legends. *Original Teaching of Cha'an Buddhism Selected from the Transmission of the Lamp* by Chang Chung-Yuang was most helpful in reporting and interpreting Chinese sayings and aphorisms. Dr. Candelaria, retired English professor from the University of Victoria, read the first draft of the story *In The Dry Woods* and Roli Gunderson of Lake Cowichan checked the correctness of the historical background.

I was greatly honoured to teach at Union Theological Seminary in Desmarinas. I fondly remember the colleagues and students who inspired the tales that were written in the Philippines. Jennifer Kelly offered astute critique of these stories while she worked on her Ph.D. in English through the University of Calgary.

A special thanks to those who knew me in New York and helped me hold it all together.

Finally, I would like to acknowledge my family. My two children, Alex and Rhiannon have always stood in the background and cheered me on. Suzanne, my elder sister, a published poet from Massachusetts, read these stories and affirmed their worth. Georgia, my younger sister, has always believed in me.

A note from the Editor:

At River Books it is customary for the editor as well as the writer to say a few words about the book. You hold in your hands the second volume we have published of Cullene Bryant's short fiction. The first volume, *Llamas in the Snow*, was one of our first titles, 'way back in 1993.

I call Cullene's narrative voice "compassionately ruthless": it combines the compassion of her day job with a relentless honesty. These at first seem to be gentle tales, in a deceptively mild voice, in a gentle and unthreatening scenery—until the tale is spun and we readers see that the landscape where we have finished is unexpectedly severe and strenuous. Our reward is in its wild unexpected beauty as well.

We're glad to welcome Cullene back to our eclectic catalogue, and hope that if you haven't read her first volume, you will have enjoyed these stories enough to go back and catch up on *Llamas*. If you're in her area, you may hear her preach, or you may hear her in her new career as a stand-up comic. She's our special Holy Fool; our Holy Fool is special. Welcome back, Cullene.

Candas Jane Dorsey
for River Books

Credits:
Some of these stories have been published, as follows:
1986 Alberta Anthology: CBC *All That Jazz*
1988 Other Voices *Waiting Hut*
1991 Negative Capability USA *Missa Solemnis*
1998 Room of One's Own *Wild Life In The Canadian Wilderness*

Biography

Cullene Bryant is a minister in the United Church of Canada and was the first female teaching hospital chaplain in the Canadian Association of Pastoral Practice and Education. Her Doctor of Ministry from Princeton was in the area of grief and loss. She has worked in hospitals in Toronto, Edmonton and New York and she has lectured as a visiting professor of pastoral theology at Union Theological Seminary in the Philippines. She studied the art of Spiritual Direction at the Center for Justice and Healing, in New York.

Bryant's first book of short fiction, *Llamas In The Snow*, was published in 1993 in Edmonton, Alberta by The Books Collective. Her short stories have aired on CBC Radio, *Alberta Anthology* and have appeared in a number of literary journals, among them *Room of One's Own* and *The Iowa Review*. She has published articles in professional magazines such as *The Journal of Pastoral Care* and *Humane Medicine*. Presently, she is completing a nonfiction manuscript, *Memoirs of a Modern Mystic: Pathways to Healing*.